R.M. U

CW01500029

ADAM DRIVER AND THE MILLION DOLLAR HAIRCUT

AQUITANIA
FIRST EDITIONS

First published in the Kingdom of the Netherlands in 2024
by Aquitania First Editions

All rights reserved

Copyright © R.M. Usatinsky 2024

Cover Design by Marina Višić
Layout by Marek Moggré

3 5 7 9 10 8 6 4 2

The moral right of R.M. Usatinsky to be identified as author of this
work has been asserted in accordance with International Law.

This is a work of fiction. All of the characters, organizations and
events portrayed in this novel either are products of the author's
imagination or are used fictitiously.

ISBN 978-1-884341-05-2

Discover more at www.rmusatinsky.com

For Michael, Jesper, Adam, Abbott and K.
Your inspiration is in every drop of ink on these pages

…and for my children

"Nothing is original. Steal from anywhere that resonates with inspiration or fuels your imagination...Select only things to steal from that speak directly to your soul. If you do this, your work (and theft) will be authentic. Authenticity is invaluable; originality is non-existent. And don't bother concealing your thievery—celebrate it if you feel like it."

–Jim Jarmusch

CHAPTER ONE

THE NIGHT BARBER

I had recently moved to the Netherlands, settling down in The Hague after having relocated there to accept a position at the International Criminal Court. Moving my family—my wife and our two teenage daughters—was more taxing this time around. This was our fourth international move in ten years and while my family was accustomed to expatriate life and genuinely enjoyed the experiences and perks that come with living abroad, this relocation was a textbook case in how whatever could go wrong did go wrong.

I woke up Monday morning to a text message from the relocation service saying that the container that our every household possession was in had been delayed at the port of Casablanca (I had been posted at the American Consulate there for the past three years) due to what I was told were "logistic issues" and it would be another three to seven days before our things arrived.

We'd been living out of our suitcases for the past week in an Airbnb as the apartment we were to move into wasn't ready due to what the realtor said were "logistic issues." So, I stumbled out of bed and, nearly killing myself on the narrowest staircase I'd ever seen, made it to the second-floor bathroom to brush my teeth before heading downstairs to join my family for breakfast. As I stood there in front of the bathroom mirror I noticed I was in desperate need of a haircut and, as I was to report at the court for my briefing in two days' time, decided to look for a barber and get the task done in short order and Google directed me to a number of barbershops in the city center though one immediately caught my attention:

The Night Barber
The Hague's First and Only After-Hours Barbershop

How peculiar, I thought to myself. An after-hours barber. Intrigued, I clicked my way over to The Night Barber's website and was even more intrigued to discover this particular barber was an American guy from Chicago (I earned my J.D. at the University of Chicago back in the 1990s and really got into the Chicagoan vibe as they are some of the coolest, most down-to-earth people you'd ever want to meet). Charlie's bio read like a work of fiction. He had played in a new wave band in Los Angeles in the 1980s; went back to college in his mid-twenties to study playwriting; got an M.A. in Education and became a teacher for twenty-five years; had been married and raised five children; and in 2017, he started a small business designing and making his own line of bow ties. It was Charlie's bow tie business that caught the attention of a master barber who had recently opened an upscale barbershop in The Hague's Royal Shopping District, just down the street from the royal palace where the Dutch king Willem Alexander conducts his official state business.

A guy came into the barbershop one day wearing a bow tie and the master barber asked where he bought it. The man said at a cooperative maker's market near the *grote kerk*. The next day, Sam, the master barber, walked over to the co-op during his lunch break and introduced himself to Charlie, who was tying a bow tie onto a mannequin head. Charlie told Sam that he was a part-time English lecturer at the hotel management school near the beach and had worn bow ties throughout his entire teaching career.

"My first teaching job," explained Charlie, "was at a children's hospital. I was a teacher's assistant at the day school which was part of the department of child psychiatry and we weren't allowed to wear neckties, for obvious safety reasons. So, I started wearing bow ties and it just kind of became my thing."

Charlie went on to say that after amassing a collection of no fewer than one hundred bow ties, some of his favorites—especially two striking navy-blue Ralph Lauren Polo bow ties—were beginning to show signs of wear. After coming across a video on YouTube of Martha Stewart making a handmade bow tie on a segment of her television program about easy-to-make homemade Christmas gifts, Charlie came up with the idea of making his own bow ties and starting a small business. Charlie went online and found a silk weaving mill in the south of England that was founded by French Huguenots in the 17th century, sending them an email telling them about his idea about starting a small bow tie business and they responded positively saying they'd be delighted to provide the fabric based on his designs. They also referred Charlie to a nearby workroom that had been making silk products for over one hundred years. Charlie wrote to them next and was delighted to receive word that the workroom— which also assembled bow ties and other silk accessories for Ralph Lauren, Paul Smith and Ted Baker—would be more than happy to help with the project.

Sam was impressed by Charlie's drive and enthusiasm about bow ties and suggested the two collaborate, Sam offering to sell Charlie's bow ties at his barbershop only asking for a couple of bow ties in return. The following Sunday, which happened to have been the Sunday before Christmas, Charlie brought over his collection and set up shop in the corner of Sam's barbershop. He proudly displayed his wares in and on an antique hutch he had brought over from Valencia, which he had purchased at the Sunday antique market next to the Mestalla soccer grounds some twenty years earlier.

After the New Year, Charlie dropped in on Sam and was overwhelmed with joy when Sam told him that he had sold fifteen bow ties in the week leading up to Christmas. Sam handed Charlie a wad of cash—seven hundred and fifty euros, to be exact—which blew Charlie's mind.

"Please," insisted Charlie. "Let me at least pay you a commission."

"That's alright," replied Sam. "I'm happy to help you start your business off on solid footing. But if you want to compensate me in some small way, you can go across the street to the Spar and buy me a couple of bananas and a croissant for lunch!"

Charlie did just that, and when he returned, he and Sam sat down on the shop's Chesterfield armchairs and got better acquainted. Charlie told Sam that he had actually worked in a hair salon when he first moved away from Chicago after graduating high school in 1981.

Charlie told Sam the story about how he moved to Los Angeles to pursue his dream of becoming a rock star. He took a few odd jobs, at first in a retail store that sold printed t-shirts and new wave regalia, then delivering pizzas until his Uncle Harry suggested he go and see his nephew, a famous Hollywood hairstylist who had a salon on Rodeo Drive in Beverly Hills. Charlie's Uncle Harry arranged a meeting with his nephew and Charlie was hired as a gopher to run errands, make coffee and sandwiches, sweep and keep the bathrooms immaculate. He was also instructed not to make eye contact or speak to any of the salon's high-profile clients (though he did have a brief conversation once with Raquel Welch, when the movie star asked Charlie where he bought the red suede Chelsea boots he'd been wearing).

Sam was inspired by Charlie's stories and infectious charisma.

"Did you ever think about getting into the business," asked Sam.

"You mean becoming a hairstylist? replied Charlie. "Not really," he continued. "I moved to L.A. with only one thing on my mind and that was getting rich and famous with my band."

Sam pondered Charlie's remarks for a moment.

"I've trained about thirty barbers," boasted Sam who, at twenty-seven was half Charlie's age. "You'd make a great barber, if only by virtue of your telling a good story and being so personable," Sam added.

"So, you're offering to train me?" asked Charlie.

"I wouldn't hesitate for a moment," replied Sam.

"Okay," said Charlie and, half in jest asked, "so, when do I start?"

Half in jest, Sam replied, "Come by next Tuesday at ten a.m."

As it turned out, Charlie found himself in the city center that following Tuesday morning as he had to pick up the new sport coat he ordered from Massimo Dutti. Remembering his playful conversation with Sam the week before, Charlie decided to pop in to the barbershop.

"Good morning Sam, here I am, ten o'clock on the dot, just like you said."

Without batting an eyelash, Sam welcomed Charlie and made the two cappuccinos as they sat once again in the brown leather Chesterfields. Sam had a feeling he might be seeing Charlie that day and just in the event that he actually showed up had prepared a couple of handmade drawings of men's faces, each section of the face highlighting a series of numbers and arrows.

"We'll start with shaving," said Sam, handing a drawing to Charlie.

"Start with shaving?" Charlie replied, his eyes wide open and mouth agape.

"You came to begin your apprenticeship, right?" asked Sam.

"Well," replied Charlie hesitatingly. "Well, sure, sure I did. We'll start with shaving."

For about an hour, Sam explained the basics of the wet shave, using the drawings and referring to a number of YouTube videos of Farzad Salehi, an Iranian barber who emigrated to Canada and became known as the "Happy Barber," opening a two-chair barbershop in downtown Vancouver's Yaletown district in 2006. Sam's family had also come to the Netherlands from Iran and according to Sam, Farzad was the best barber in the business and that I could learn a lot from watching his videos.

After a coffee break, Sam sat in one of his antique Koken barber chairs and instructed Charlie to set up the station, prep him for a shave and pick up the straight razor shavette that was sitting atop of the workstation on a clean, perfectly folded black cotton towel.

"Show me how you would hold the razor," said Sam.

Charlie proceeded to pick up the shavette, open it and slide it between his fingers. Impressed, Sam asked where he had learned how to shave. To Sam's surprise, Charlie said he had never actually used a straight razor but had seen them used hundreds of times in films, TV shows and at Ross Barbershop back in the old neighborhood on Chicago's North Side. Charlie spent a good part of his childhood there accompanying his father, grandfather and great-grandfather who would all get shaves and haircuts every Friday afternoon before Shabbos when Charlie was young boy.

Sam instructed Charlie to go through the motions of how he thought a shave should be executed. Charlie lathered up the shaving brush with a thick coat of foamy gel on Sam's face and neck and—with the bladeless shavette—proceeded to simulate a shave. After just three strokes, Sam put his hand up.

"Alright," he said, removing the towel from his chest and wiping off the gel. Charlie stood there somewhat taken aback (did he do something wrong? he thought to himself). "Try again," instructed Sam. "Go ahead, lather me up from the beginning." Charlie didn't say a word and followed Sam's instructions, wetting the brush and re-applying a thick layer of shaving gel. "Now," said Sam, "open up the top drawer and you'll see a small box that says Derby on it. Open the box and remove a blade."

"Remove a blade," said Charlie nervously.

"Remove a blade and insert it into the shavette. And don't forget to snap off the corner like in the video before you put it in."

"You said I wouldn't be using a real blade until Sunday," Charlie said, removing the paper wrapper from the blade.

"What day is it today?" asked Sam, with a hint of whimsy in his voice.

"It's Tuesday," answered Charlie.

"That's close enough for jazz," continued Sam. "Now, let's get started on that shave."

For the next ninety minutes, Sam reclined in the barber chair with a little smirk, as calm and collected as if he were lounging poolside at some tropical resort. Meanwhile, Charlie slowly and meticulously shaved Sam without as much as even a single nick.

"Pretty impressive," said Sam, moving the handheld mirror closer to his face. "For a beginner, that is! Now you only need to shave ninety-nine more faces—and do a hundred haircuts—and you'll be ready to become the best professional barber in The Hague; well, second best anyway."

That was Charlie's first day as an apprentice, and by the time he picked up his daughters from school later that afternoon, he was totally exhausted and fell asleep on the couch before dinner.

I made my first appointment with the after-hours barber that Monday evening at eleven o'clock, figuring if I was going to get the full experience, why not take the last appointment of the evening? After dinner, we sat around watching TV and I guess I had dozed off when my wife tapped me on the shoulder telling me she was going upstairs to bed. Half asleep, I remembered my appointment and told my wife I'd be going out to the barbershop in about half an hour. She looked at me as she snickered and shook her head, still trying to get a grasp of the idea that anyone would actually go for a haircut in the middle of the night, as she put it.

I arrived in the quaint little square named after Anna Pavlovna (Paulowna in Dutch), the Russian-born Queen of the Netherlands through her marriage to King William II, about a ten-minute walk from our Airbnb and not much further away than our soon-to-be new apartment nearby. The square was dotted with sidewalk cafés, bistros and wine bars surrounded by lush trees whose leaves danced in the trickles of moonlight that shone through quickly moving clouds.

And there it was, The Night Barber, a small storefront with a vintage wooden sign hanging from the 1930s-era cream brick building, painted in antique black with bright white letters that were both bold and welcoming, a glow of warm lights emanating from inside the shop.

I walked inside and was greeted by Charlie, who looked much younger than I had imagined, especially after reading his website bio which said he was, in fact, a retired teacher. He certainly didn't look like any retired person I'd ever known and I was greeted with a warm welcome and a hearty sincere handshake.

"You must be my eleven o'clock," said Charlie, gesturing for me to take a seat in his large black tufted barber chair.

"Yes, I'm Casper," I replied, "I made an appointment this morning on your website."

"Casper," repeated Charlie. "Like the ghost?" he added, playfully.

"Well," I said, "like Casper, Wyoming, actually."

As the barber tucked my shirt collar in and, in a dramatic swish, wrapped me in a smooth black cape with a large white logo, I explained I was named after Casper, Wyoming.

"My father's family were early settlers there during the oil boom in the late 19th century," I told the barber as he listened attentively while reaching for a comb and spray bottle.

Over the next forty-five minutes, Charlie indulged me with one of the best haircuts I'd ever had, engaging conversation set to an amazing playlist of 80s new wave music and a dram of the most delicious chrysanthemum and honey liqueur from a distillery in, of all places, Chicago. But the one thing that stood out most was Charlie's effortless ability to tell a story in a way I've never heard anyone tell a story before. It was completely and authentically engaging, and he made me feel as if I were part of the story, experiencing exactly what he had been talking about. It's hard to explain really, because I'd simply never felt so deeply connected to a storyteller before. I asked him how it was he came to be The Night Barber, and he told the story as I explained it a few pages back. I mean, it's all so fairly simple and straightforward, but the way Charlie told it was so, so captivating, and before I knew it he was removing the cape and dusting my neck and forehead with a delightfully fragrant talcum powder that reminded me of how my father smelled when he came back from his weekly visit to the barbershop when I was a boy.

I paid and thanked Charlie for a wonderful experience, telling him I'd found my new barber in The Hague, and that I'd be back in four weeks to see him again. He shook my hand, thanked me and told me he appreciated my giving him a try saying he knew there were many good barbers in town I could have chosen.

"Not one that would have cut my hair at eleven o'clock at night," I said.

"No, I suppose not," replied Charlie, opening the door for me as I stepped out into the moonlit square, all the better for the pleasurable experience I'd just had.

Needless to say, I became one of Charlie the barber's regular customers. I'd book in about every four weeks for a haircut and, once I decided to let my beard grow out again (at my wife and daughter's behest), for what Charlie called his *deluxe combo*, which was a haircut, shampoo and an exquisite beard trim that included a hot steam, lemon and eucalyptus oil facial, something I'd never experienced before and now can't fathom having lived without it all my life. If you have any degree of facial hair and happen to find yourself in The Hague one day, definitely book one of these treatments (you can thank me later!).

We finally moved into our new apartment and settled into new surroundings. I was assigned to head up investigations into the ongoing crimes against humanity cases brought before the International Criminal Court concerning the Republic of the Philippines during their so-called "war on drugs" campaign occurring between 2011 and 2019. Our twin daughters were enrolled at a private international school and my wife continued working on her doctoral degree in sociology that she began nearly a decade earlier and was, as she puts it, "on the verge of finishing". As work kept me busy and frequently traveling to the Philippines, I found both camaraderie and repose at Charlie's barbershop and looked forward to my monthly visits, not so much for the haircut and beard trim—which were wonderful on their own—but to enjoy the company of a kindred spirit and catch up on where Charlie left off his last story. During a previous visit, I asked Charlie where his obsession with 80s new wave music came from. He told me about the time he spent playing in a new wave band in the 1980s out in Los Angeles, and his love for the genre never waned. He was a virtual walking encyclopedia of new wave music and could recite every lyric, knew all the songs and the bands and band members who recorded them and every anecdote and backstory to what was a truly magnificent decade of popular music.

Charlie founded his band, Café Society, shortly after arriving in L.A. in the summer of 1982. He had recently joined a gym on Ventura Boulevard in Encino, and was there one afternoon when he observed two young guys sitting on a free weight bench sharing headphones and listening to something on their Walkman. Charlie approached the guys who were seemingly in a trance as one swayed while the other air-drummed to whatever they were listening to. Charlie asked if they were musicians and they said they were and had taken a break from their workout to listen to some demos of musicians they were considering for their new band. They had just parted ways with their lead singer and guitarist—the two guys played bass and drums and had recently taken on a keyboard player—and as they had some gigs lined up for later that summer, they were scrambling to find some new bandmates. Intrigued and interested, Charlie introduced himself and said he was both a singer and guitarist who had just been fronting a three-piece punk band in Phoenix, where he had been living for the past nine months, coaxed by Burton Korer, a former bandmate, from his short time playing with Rob Simon's band during high school back in Chicago. Burt was a year older and had moved with his family to Scottsdale after graduation and had convinced Charlie to come to Phoenix and start a band before going to L.A. Charlie agreed as he had some time to kill before his girlfriend would be graduating from high school and meeting Charlie in L.A. after graduation in June 1982.

The guys were definitely intrigued by Charlie's story and asked if he'd like to come over to the drummer's house and jam. Charlie agreed but thought they should hear some of his songs first saying he had a six-song demo he had recorded at Camelback Studios in Phoenix earlier that year outside in his car's glove compartment and he went out to the parking lot to fetch it. Charlie returned with his cassette in hand and the guys popped the demo into the Walkman and loved what they heard. They turned to each other and then to Charlie saying to forget about coming over to jam and just calling it their first rehearsal. Ron, the drummer, lived minutes away from the gym and Charlie followed him up the hill that led to the Clark Gable Estates and to the house where Ron lived with his general practitioner father, mother, two brothers and sister. Charlie found the house to be palatial and somewhat ostentatious, and though he had spent many summers in L.A. visiting family who all had huge houses with pools and two-car garages, he'd never been inside a house quite as extravagant as Ron's. And if Charlie was impressed with Ron's opulent house, he was equally impressed by his drum kit, which was previously owned by Genesis and Phil Collins' touring drummer Chester Thompson, who played that beautiful, orange, double-kick Pearl drum set on their last world tour. Thompson was a patient of Ron's fathers and sold the kit to Ron for a song.

As it was summertime, Ron suggested the three take a dip in the pool before setting up their instruments (Charlie would play the vintage 1968 Fender Stratocaster that belonged to Ron's best friend Tony). While Charlie was enjoying a swim and the view overlooking the San Fernando Valley, Ron went inside for some drinks and chips but popped his head out of the sliding patio door to ask Charlie if he'd ever seen MTV. Charlie had heard about the all-music-video channel that debuted the previous year on cable, but as he didn't own a television set, he had never seen this new MTV that seemed to be all the rage. Ron signaled for Charlie and Craig, the bass player, to come running and check out this new video by a British band The Fixx. Charlie stood in the open patio door and saw his first music video *Saved by Zero*, which made a huge impression on the budding rock star. From that moment on, Charlie knew exactly what he wanted to be and he seemed to be in the right place for executing his plan.

Charlie got a job working at a boutique in the Valley where his great aunt worked. He sold women's shoes and accessories five days a week and would rehearse every night with his new band. The guys got off to a great start and soon found a keyboard player, Matt, who would later go on to form the band Under the Sun in the late 1980s and that was signed to the prestigious Magna Carta progressive rock label.

Rehearsals took place in Ron's seldom-used formal dining room, his family enjoying the music their son and his band were making so much they would often invite friends over for impromptu living room or backyard concerts. Ron's younger teenage sister was also a big fan and could be seen peeking out of her bedroom door, most often at Charlie, who it was obvious she had a crush on. She was only thirteen, but already had an older boyfriend who she had been seeing for a while and who was allowed to spend nights at the family home. She even kept a massive supply of condoms in her en suite bathroom, provided courtesy of her doctor father.

The band came together quickly and they were ready to record a demo and start looking for gigs. They recorded six songs at a studio in Los Angeles, run by an Asian-American sound engineer named Clive. The band recorded all the basic tracks in one go and returned two more times, once for vocals and overdubs and once for the final mix. It was only the second time Charlie had recorded in a professional studio, but he was in his element and gave the impression of having much more recording experience than he actually did. After the band approved the final mix, they had a couple dozen cassettes made and turned them over to Charlie's cousin Ross, who was the band's self-appointed manager. Ross, or Sol as Charlie called him, managed to get the tapes into the right people's hands and the band was soon booked to play their first handful of gigs.

Café Society's first live performance was an opening slot at the famous Madame Wong's in Chinatown, where Charlie's heroes The Police played one of their first ever shows in the United States in May of 1979. I've actually seen a photo of The Police playing that gig and it's on the same stage as the photo Charlie showed me of his band playing on what is unmistakably the exact same stage in the exact same venue, right down to the bamboo slats and overhead stage lights.

By the fall, the band was playing three or four gigs a week. And while they couldn't break through the competition of longer-lived headlining bands, they did gain quite a reputation for being a reliable opening and closing act in support of the more better-known bands on the L.A. circuit. One such band was the Red Hot Chili Peppers, whose lead singer Anthony Kiedis introduced Café Society as "the best opening band in L.A." But that almost never would have come to pass had it not been for one of Charlie's other favorite bands, Chicago, and his determination to be the first local new wave band in L.A. to have a three-piece horn section. That's what Kiedis and legions of other bands who were now wanting Café Society to open up for them considered cool and innovative for the times. And for Charlie's desire of actually putting together a horn section in the band, he had to overcome one small obstacle…getting rid of the band's keyboard player.

Charlie had always dreamed of incorporating real horns into the band to create a wall of sound that other bands thinly were creating with the use of synthesizers. Not that Charlie didn't like synths. He actually loved the parts Matt created to fill the empty spaces of his songs, but felt having a horn section—especially for live gigs—would really set the band apart from the field and capture the attention (and hopefully the interest) of the record label A&R people who frequented the clubs looking to sign new talent. But Matt wasn't convinced and felt that this was simply a way for Charlie to push him out of the band. It didn't help that the band had rejected the idea of Matt singing lead on some of the songs and bringing his own material into the group which was agreed by the others of not really fitting in to the Café Society sound. After some infighting and a few awkward conversations, Matt quit the band and the others agreed to carry on and simply find a new keyboard player; they also agreed to Charlie's idea of a horn section and left it up to him to get that going.

Charlie had a friend from work who played bass in another local band. Vince told Charlie about a guy named Dave Cushman, a trumpet player and arranger who had arranged some saxophone parts for Vince's band. It turned out that Dave lived just up the street from where Charlie was living in Tarzana, so he dropped by his house one evening and introduced himself. Cushman lived in a detached, single-family house with an overgrown front garden and window frames that needed a fresh coat of paint. Charlie was invited in and Cushman introduced him to his mother, with whom he shared the ranch-style house. Cushman led Charlie into his bedroom, which doubled as his studio. Charlie immediately noticed how the room had not one, but two window air-conditioning units seemingly each on full blast. Cushman said he couldn't bear the L.A. heat and used the air-conditioners year-round. Also catching Charlie's attention were the hundreds of empty 7-11 Big Gulp cups that were stacked dozens high and strewn all over Cushman's uncomfortably cold bedroom. Cushman was an imposing character, heavyset and disheveled, but Charlie was convinced he had found the right person to create the horn charts he needed. Not ever having studied formally meant that Charlie could neither read or write music and Cushman was patient as he listened—for hours—as Charlie would hum his ideas for horn parts over the songs as they played over Cushman's studio monitors. In the end, it took Cushman about a month to transcribe all of Charlie's ideas and when Charlie returned, Cushman handed him three glossy yellow folders with the horn charts—for trumpet, tenor saxophone and trombone— inside. Charlie paid Cushman for his work, and as he was leaving he handed Charlie a piece of paper with the names of some horn players he thought might be a good fit for Charlie's new wave band. Once he got home, Charlie started going through the list and calling the horn players that Cushman had recommended.

The first person on the list was a female trumpet player named Anne. Charlie liked the idea of a female in the band and he called her, delighted that the short telephone conversation ended with Anne agreeing to meet the band at their next rehearsal to see if there was some chemistry. Before hanging up with Charlie, she mentioned the name of a friend Dan, who played trombone and gave him Dan's number. Charlie thanked Anne and hung up the phone and immediately called Dan who, like Anne, was excited to see what Café Society was all about and also agreed to show up at the band's next rehearsal. In turn, Dan told Charlie to give his saxophonist friend Jeff a call. Dan said knowing Jeff, he'd jump at the chance to play in an original pop band as he had grown tired of playing in cover bands. Charlie called Jeff and while he was definitely interested— especially knowing that his friends Anne and Dan might be involved—he told Charlie that he had just signed on to substitute for a friend on a cruise ship gig and wouldn't be available for the next three weeks. With the band's next rehearsal just four days away, Charlie decided to place a free ad in the classifieds of a local entertainment guide and, to his surprise, got a phone call from an interested saxophone player the very next day. Charlie invited the sax player over to his apartment the next evening to talk and to play the guy the band's demo.

The next evening, the sax player, Cornelius, arrived at Charlie's apartment. Charlie invited him in, poured some soft drinks and popped his demo into the cassette deck. Cornelius immediately liked the songs and asked to see the saxophone charts. Removing the charts from their shiny yellow folders, Cornelius laughed and told Charlie he couldn't play them. How was that possible? Charlie thought to himself. Cornelius said the charts were for tenor saxophone, and he played alto! Cornelius said he'd love to play with the band but the sax charts would have to be transcribed, so Charlie would again have to rely on the services of Dave Cushman who, Charlie thought, wouldn't be so keen to see him again so soon. So, who was this Cornelius and how did it come to pass that he was so eager to get playing with this local band of kids who were barely out of their teens? Cornelius had a story to tell and Charlie wasn't even prepared for what he was about to be told. Cornelius wasn't exactly who Charlie had expected would be someone to answer an ad in a free weekly. He stood over six feet tall, was a large-built African American with a slightly unkempt afro and was soft-spoken and kind. He was also, in Charlie's estimation, at least fifteen years (or more) older than Charlie.

Cornelius Bumpus had most recently played with the Doobie Brothers and had left the band a few months earlier to be replaced by various touring musicians. He had also released his first solo album a year earlier and, as he told Charlie, had recently moved to L.A. and was looking to get involved with a different kind of vibe, some younger musicians that were doing something completely different than he had been accustomed to. Of course, Charlie had heard of the Doobie Brothers; they had some major hits in the 70s like *Listen to the Music*, *Long Train Runnin'*, *China Grove*, *Black Water*, and *What a Fool Believes*, all in the top 20. Cornelius even composed and sang *Thank You Love* on the Doobie Brothers' platinum-selling 1980 release *One Step Closer*. So, it turned out the guy sitting in Charlie's living room was in a famous rock band—a legendary rock band—and was now interested in playing new wave music with a bunch of young guys who were barely out of high school (Craig and Ron were actually *still* in high school!). While Charlie couldn't quite get his head around that idea, he was cautiously optimistic about the possibilities and opportunities having a guy like Cornelius in the band could offer. After Cornelius left, Charlie had a walk over to Dave Cushman's house and told him about his chance encounter with Cornelius Bumpus (who Cushman had of course heard of and was wary about the story Charlies had just told him about meeting the famous saxophonist). Nevertheless, Cushman agreed to modify the charts—at a nominal cost—and get them back to Charlie in a day or two.

The next band rehearsal—which would be the first Cornelius would participate in—was a few days later and while Charlie had informed everyone that a new sax player would be on hand, he deliberately didn't tell anyone *who* that sax player was. And in dramatic fashion, Cornelius Bumpus was the last person to arrive at rehearsal that night and when Charlie introduced him, there was a long silence followed by eyes nearly popping out of sockets and mouths falling agape onto the floor. That first rehearsal with the full band went very well and they all went out for pizza afterwards to talk about their plans for the next round of gigs. Also present that evening was Charlie's friend, Scott Metcalfe, who was filling in on keyboards until a permanent synthesizer player was found. And that happened just a few days later at the band's next rehearsal.

Charlie's girlfriend Sari had moved to L.A. at summer's end as Charlie was in the early stages of putting the band together. They had been together since they were teenagers and Sari loved Charlie's music and being around the various bands he'd played in back in Chicago, and she was certainly enjoying seeing how things were coming along so nicely for Café Society. Sari came to every rehearsal and gig and was their biggest fan (and their best—and only—roadie!). She sat in their bedroom in the small two-room apartment she and Charlie rented in Tarzana while he worked diligently writing songs for the band in his free time. One night at a rehearsal in the new drummer Lee's garage, while the band went inside the house to take a break, they were suddenly surprised to hear the sound of Scott's Roland Juno-60 keyboard coming from the garage. Stranger still, Scott was sitting at Lee's kitchen table drinking a Coke. Charlie and the others set their drinks down and all walked out back to the garage to find Sari playing *Other Men* on the keyboard. It turned out that Sari, who had taken piano lessons as a young girl, knew every keyboard part to every song her boyfriend had written. Scott, whose tenure in the band was temporary until a full-time keyboardist was brought on board walked over to Charlie and said, "I guess you've found your keyboard player." And Scott was right, indeed they had. Scott even sold the Juno 60 to Charlie for a fraction of what he paid for it saying, "Consider it my investment in what's going to become the hottest band in L.A."

Charlie mentioned, though only briefly without going into much detail, that Scott later went on to work in the film industry and passed away in February 2017. It did, however, take some coaxing to convince Sari to fill the role of new wave keyboard player, but she quickly and confidently came unto her own and found her place in the band, which was now a seven-piece, horn-toting new wave band, a band whose likes had not yet been seen on the L.A. club circuit.

This new Café Society was the band that appealed to people like Howie Hubberman, who nearly got the band signed to a major record label. In the summer of 1984 Hubberman offered them the opening slot for Bang-Bang's *Life Part II* record release gig and party at the Troubadour on the Sunset Strip. Bang-Bang, touted to become the next big thing, was a new romantic hybrid that sounded like Culture Club and looked like Duran Duran. They broke up shortly after their debut although their music video for their single *This is Love* on heavy rotation on MTV. As an opening band, Café Society were usually the last band to soundcheck, meaning that the other bands had already done theirs and had left the venue to get dinner or drinks. But bands like the Chili Peppers, T.S.O.L., Black Flag, The Minutemen, Meat Puppets and Los Lobos would always hang around to hear Café Society's soundcheck because they loved the sound and thought the horns were amazing.

Cornelius Bumpus only did a handful of shows with Café Society and went on to release another solo album and a record with his trio. He also worked with Donald Fagen and toured with Fagen's band Steely Dan. Interestingly enough, Café Society horn players Jeff (who later joined on saxophone) and Anne, later went on to play with the L.A.-based Steely Dan Tribute band, Dr. Wu, and continued playing dozens of shows each year. Cornelius Bumpus died in February 2004 after suffering a heart attack while aboard a flight from New York to California. The plane made an emergency landing in Sioux City, Iowa, but the larger-than-life saxophonist from Santa Cruz,

California died before the plane ever landed. Cornelius Bumpus was 58.

But those aren't the only claims to fame the original horn players can lay claim to. Brooklyn-born, New York City-based trombonist Dan Levine played, toured and recorded with some of the greatest names in contemporary music: Bruce Springsteen, Frank Sinatra, Ray Charles, Liza Minelli, Rufus Wainwright and Bjork, to name a few. Trumpeter Anne King's musical résumé is equally as impressive as she has played with dozens of stars over the past four decades such as Rod Stewart, Guns 'N Roses, Adele, k.d. lang and Don Henley. Jeff Dellisanti also kept his saxophone reeds moist over the years by playing in a number of well-known tribute bands as well as performing with Rikki Lee Jones and The Young Dubliners. He also played on a new Café Society single, *Daylight Storm,* that Charlie wrote and recorded in The Hague in 2020 with Paraguayan drummer Christian Palmieri and Russian bassist Andrey Zakharov. Jeff recorded his saxophone solos remotely (as did guest keyboardist and mixing producer Jason Soudah), and through the magic of the internet they were added to the final mix that was mastered at the legendary Abbey Road Studios in London. It was the first official Café Society song released since the band's formation in 1982. "It took 38 years to release to my first single," Charlie said. Better late than never.

I loved the stories about his band and all the relationships he forged during those years he spent in L.A. and in Phoenix, which is where it all started, with his old bandmate from Chicago, Burton Korer who played the Fender Rhodes and Moog eggshell synth in Rob Simon's band with Dave Rubin on drums (Dave worked at the kosher deli where Charlie's father was the night manager), and Eugene Canning, the bassist, who passed away in 2016. Eugene also played bass in Charlie's first real band Strange Magic that he started with his boyhood friend Todd Berns and drummer Tony Ryan. Tony was later replaced by Sari's brother Perry who today owns one of Chicago's most respected private detective agencies, founded in 1959 by his father, a British immigrant from Hull, England.

Charlie first met Sari at a 4H event in Chicago where, at ages 14 and 13 respectively, they were competing in a public speaking contest. Charlie won the first-place blue ribbon while Sari came in second, winning the red. It would be another year before the two would meet again at the Henry N. Hart JCC, where they were part of the Junior Henry Street Players theater company. I love how Charlie described the first day Sari arrived to join the company and how he reminisced about their early relationship's ups and downs…

There was a buzz in the rehearsal room that day, everyone talking about 'Sari this and Sari that'. And while I'd met her a year earlier, I didn't remember her name, so when she showed up for our first rehearsal that afternoon, I was pleasantly surprised. She was stunning, with straight, long chocolate brown hair and deeply tanned skin that made her large white teeth seem all the brighter (she had just that very day returned from her family's summer vacation in Florida). She was wearing an orange terrycloth sundress that revealed every curve and detail of her body. Cliché as it sounds, it was love at first sight and by the end of the summer we were officially boyfriend and girlfriend. Sari came from an orthodox Jewish family and wasn't allowed to go out on Friday nights or Saturdays, as her family strictly observed the sabbath. So, I'd spend Friday night dinners with Sari's family and come back for lunch after shul on Saturday afternoon, where Sari and I would play board games and pool and make out in the family's finished basement. She attended the Jewish high school and as she was a year younger, she was a year behind me in school. Once I graduated from high school in June of 1981, Sari and I made a pact that once she graduated the following June, she would join me in Los Angeles, and it worked out just as we had planned. During the year we were apart, I'm somewhat ashamed to say that I wasn't exactly faithful. I had recently turned 18 and not that I was looking for them, opportunities seemed to just come my way. First, it was Jill, an old classmate from grammar school who moved away before we graduated. We kept in touch and I'd see her mother from time to time as she was a clerk at our local post office who was there the day I went to register for the draft on my eighteenth birthday and handed me the forms. My mother had called me in Scottsdale one evening to tell me she had run into Jill at the post office and she asked about me. My mother filled her in on all the details and Jill asked if she could have my phone number as she was thinking about doing some traveling and perhaps would come to Arizona to pay me a visit. Jill called me a few days later to say she had gotten my number from my mother and asked if she could come out and see me. She told me that the boy she'd been dating had recently been killed in a plane crash and that she was going through one of the worst moments of her life. I told her she was more than welcome to come and she thanked me and said she would try to make plans soon and get back to me. A month or so later, I found myself picking Jill up from Sky Harbor Airport. On the drive back *to my apartment in Scottsdale, she thanked me and told me she was on the pill, which I thought was a strange thing to tell me though it did peak my interest. Jill ended up spending a few months with me, but her sadness turned into late night drinking binges that, in turn, became daytime binges and by the time I arrived home from my skip tracing job in a trailer on a lot in Phoenix, she was already beyond consolation and in no condition to do much of anything. To add to the bizarre story of my last few months in Scottsdale, my boss, a guy named Rick, moved into my spare room when his wife discovered him cheating with one of our clients who worked at an insurance company in Houston, and threw him out. Jill ended up living with Rick in his room for the remainder of the time she was in Arizona, and we didn't speak again for another 25 years. A few years after we re-connected, Jill bravely fought breast cancer and remains cancer free to this day. After her divorce and raising two sons, she has also found a new partner and seems happier than I'd ever known her to be. After Jill went back to Chicago, I was approached one night after a gig I'd done with Burt in Phoenix. We'd put together a punk trio with a lesbian drummer we met named Monique and were playing the sarsaparilla bar circuit (because we were underage and not allowed to play in venues that served alcohol). Judy was twenty-five, tall and lanky with a head of curly brown hair. And visibly pregnant. She came up to me to tell me how much she enjoyed our set and asked if I wanted to take her home. I remember actually laughing so hard when she asked me that, the cream soda I'd been drinking came up through my nose. She laughed it off as she saw I was a bit embarrassed, but she gently touched my shoulder and reached over and kissed my cheek. I suppose you could say that was the first time I'd ever had a one-night stand, but it* was certainly an experience I've never forgotten. I never got her phone number (uncertain if I would have called) and I never saw her again. Finally, there was Misty. For as long as I had worked at the skip tracing agency, I was in daily contact with the local credit bureau we were subscribed to. They helped us by sharing credit information and personal details about the deadbeats we were trying to find. Misty had the most beautiful, seductive voice I'd ever heard and one day I gathered up the nerve to ask her over for dinner. Misty arrived and when she rang my doorbell I peeked out of the peephole and to my surprise what I saw was a very overweight, very dark-skinned, black-haired Latina. I invited her in and she handed me a bottle of red wine and immediately began kissing me passionately on the mouth, then pushing me onto the couch as she began undoing the belt on my 501s. Needless to say, my experiences in Arizona those short nine months were nothing short of incredible, though there wasn't a moment through any of it that I didn't feel terribly guilty for being unfaithful to Sari. But the Misty story doesn't end there. After dinner—I broiled fish and red potatoes—we were right back on the couch and she couldn't keep her hands to herself, insisting I was the love of her life and saying she wanted to be the mother of my children. And just before she had the opportunity to give that another try, my doorbell rang. I couldn't possibly imagine who that could have been at my door, especially that late on a weeknight and to my utter surprise it was Burt—with Rob Simon, who had flown in from Chicago that afternoon—coming to pay me a visit. I totally freaked out and told Misty not to make a sound as I decided I would pretend as if I wasn't home. They rang the bell for about fifteen minutes thinking I had to be home before giving up and walking away. Then, about ten minutes later, they called from a *nearby payphone. I was simply too embarrassed for my friends to have seen me with Misty. My time in Phoenix was capped off with Burt taking me to see a local band, The Jetzons, at Merlyn's in Tempe. I'd never been to a club that was so packed and when the band took the stage the crowd flew into a frenzy, bobbing and swaying to the pulsating rhythms of what was the best band I'd seen up until that point in my life (well, maybe the best band next to Special Affect back in Chicago). By the time they played their hit song 'You' that was high up on the local charts, the audience was electrified and even I, who wasn't much of a dancer, couldn't help but sway and bob like the rest of the audience. This was a monumental moment for me as a young musician and one that would be the catalyst for my moving out of the slowly waning punk rock movement to the synthesizer-powered, clean beat drive of new wave.*

At the beginning of June 1982, Charlie sold his Kawasaki KZ650 and rented a car to get him, his dog and the few belongings he owned to Los Angeles. Arriving in L.A., Charlie rented a one-bedroom apartment on Arch Drive in Studio City, and spent his days looking for jobs and sitting by the pool with a collection of neighbors who were all industry people—actors, showgirls, technicians—even a guy who claimed to have had a short stint as one of the last Marlboro Men to appear in a television commercial.

Charlie started working at the shoe shop, playing with the band and getting ready for Sari to arrive in a few weeks' time. A year later, in June of 1983, Sari decided to throw Charlie a surprise twentieth birthday party at his aunt and uncle's house in Woodland Hills. She invited family, friends from work and, of course, the guys in the band. And because she was a kind and empathetic person, she invited Ron's younger sister Tema to the party, feeling badly for the girl whose boyfriend had recently dumped her for another girl. After the party, Charlie and his bandmates agreed to meet up at a local club to see a few bands and Sari asked Charlie to drive Tema back to her parents' house before meeting the others at the club, and of course he agreed. What Charlie could have never imaged would happen, happened as Tema asked Charlie if he wouldn't mind taking a detour and stopping for a few minutes to talk and look out over the Valley from high up on Mulholland Drive, known popularly as Lovers' Lane. Charlie parked his car in a turnout and Tema threw herself at him, kissing him passionately while maneuvering herself on top of him. That night, Charlie never made it to the club, but ended back at Ron's house and into his sister's bed, where he spent the next few hours, only going home as the sun was coming up over the Valley. Charlie and Tema would see each other as often as possible. They would have intimate rendezvous in her bathroom while Sari was just feet away (the bathroom off the living room where the band rehearsed had a second door connected directly to Tema's bedroom). She would often open the door and peak out signaling for Charlie to come. In the end, Sari found out about Charlie and Tema and gave Charlie an ultimatum: that he never stepped foot into Ron's house again or move out of their apartment. By then, tensions were beginning to mount with the squabbles over Charlie's wanting to bring horns into the band and Ron often siding with Matt. In a fairly drastic move, Charlie convinced Craig to move on from Ron and Matt and look for a new drummer and keyboard player. While Ron and Craig had been boyhood friends, he chose to take a new direction and parted company with Ron and Matt, putting his trust in Charlie, whose music he liked playing and felt there was more of a future with Charlie. Matt was never seen or heard from again and Ron was killed, along with his best friend Tony (whose vintage Strat Charlie played at many live gigs and recording sessions), when the small plane he was piloting crashed in the Sand Canyon area of the Santa Clarita Valley in July 2009. Ron Weiss was just forty-three years old.

One day at work, Charlie asked his friend Vince, the one who would later recommend horn arranger Dave Cushman, if he knew any drummers looking for a band. Coincidentally, Vince's band had recently been auditioning new drummers and he told Charlie about a guy named Lee Coltman, who he really liked but his bandmates voted against him for another drummer. Charlie called Lee and he and Craig met him one evening at the gym where Lee taught gymnastics and had been given permission by the owners to keep his drums in a back room where he could practice after hours. The three hit it off immediately and Charlie couldn't help but notice how much Lee looked like—and played drums like—his favorite drummer Stewart Copeland of The Police. Café Society had their new drummer, and with Charlie's friend Scott Metcalfe on board to fill in temporarily on keyboards, they moved into Lee's garage in Chatsworth and began rehearsal in earnest. Sari moved into the keyboard player's role and the horns were incorporated soon thereafter; it was time to take the new and improved Café Society on the road. After the band's first live show with horns—featuring former Doobie Brothers saxophonist Cornelius Bumpus—at FM Station in North Hollywood, the band starting using the board mixes made at shows as their new demo and calling card. And the gigs started rolling in. Café Society managed to remain a band until 1986, when things began to unravel and Craig and Lee began losing faith in Charlie's ability—or lack thereof—of taking the band to the next level. While the band was gigging regularly and Charlie was pleased with the status quo, both Craig and Lee thought Charlie could be doing more, being more *ambitious,* as they both remarked.

Charlie and Sari had been broken up for about a year by the time Craig told Charlie that he was leaving the band. Lee agreed to stay on and was pleased at Charlie bringing keyboardist Ken Lee, a friend of Charlie's cousin Ross, into the band. Craig was replaced by bassist Jon Grimson, a Chicagoan who studied bass at the prestigious Berklee College of Music, who came highly recommended by the Chili Pepper's guitarist Hillel Slovak. Charlie and Israeli-born Slovak became friends as they had their Jewish upbringing in common and ran into each other frequently at gigs and at the savings and loan where Charlie worked on Fairfax Avenue, where Charlie had another soon-to-be famous customer, Johnny Depp, who was also part of the local band scene trying to make a name for himself as a musician. Depp's first wife, Lori Allison, would come in to the bank regularly to manage the young couple's affairs, until one day Johnny accompanied her. Charlie and Johnny immediately recognized each other from the clubs and Johnny was pleasantly surprised to discover the nice bank teller his wife always spoke so highly of was actually Charlie. Soon before leaving his job at the bank, Lori and Johnny came in late one morning and stood by waiting for Charlie's window to become free. Lori handed Charlie a check for twenty-five thousand dollars made payable to her husband. She said she was glad that her husband had taken her advice and pursued television and movie roles as she was convinced it was on film where Johnny would get the best exposure and had the greatest chance of achieving the fame and fortune he most desired. The check was Johnny's fee for his role in Wes Craven's *A Nightmare on Elm Street*, Depp's film debut and breakout role as Springwood High School student Glen Lantz. While Charlie was processing the couple's deposit, Johnny leaned over and whispered into Lori's ear. "Johnny's come up with a great idea," said Lori, taking the deposit receipt from Charlie. "Why don't you join us for lunch across the street at Canter's, we'll make it a celebration, and since you've been so good to us since we opened our account here, we figured the least we could to show our appreciation is invite you to join us for a pastrami sandwich!"

Charlie closed his teller window and walked out from behind the counter. He told his supervisor, Rudy Membreno, that he was going to lunch. Then he and the Depps walked over to Canter's for a delightful meal while Johnny talked about his plans to try and put another band together and his excitement of landing an audition for an upcoming new film written and directed by Oliver Stone. Johnny would eventually audition for the film and earn the role of Lerner, a small part in Stone's 1986 Vietnam War blockbuster, *Platoon*.

For the past year—since Charlie's breakup with Sari—he'd been spending more time in Chicago, where he found the support of friends who helped him get over the heartbreak of the end of his long relationship. Returning to Los Angeles at the beginning of 1987, he told Lee, Ken and

Craig, who by that time had convinced Charlie to let him back in the band, that he'd be leaving L.A. for good at the end of the spring and going back to Chicago to sort out the next chapter of his life. During Charlie's final months in L.A., he, Craig, Lee and Ken recorded one final demo—well, at least one final demo in *English*—at a studio in Hollywood. A few years later, in the summer of 1991, on a trip to Los Angeles to attend a family wedding, Charlie called Craig and Lee and asked if they'd be interested in recording some Spanish songs Charlie had written during the two years he had lived in Granada, Spain. The three—accompanied by Charlie's Spanish fiancée—met at Charlie's favorite restaurant, Thai Cottage on Ventura Boulevard in Studio City. Charlie ate there almost every week and would often coincide with Molly Ringwald and Dweezil Zappa who always said hello. He dined there regularly over the years and more frequently when he moved back to his first apartment complex on Arch Drive where he rented the newly-renovated one-bedroom where the Marlboro Man and his boyfriend once lived. After a meal of beef and chicken satay skewers, squid in fresh mint, white rice, heaps of peanut sauce and Thai iced tea, the four went to a converted guesthouse, now recording studio, in Sherman Oaks. They recorded the seven songs Charlie had written in Spanish with Craig on bass and Lee playing an assortment of percussion instruments while Charlie laid down two tracks of guitars, vocals and vocal harmonies. The session went on until the early hours of the morning though Craig and Lee had gone home while Charlie remained behind to finish the overdubs and mixing. That was the last time Charlie, Craig and Lee would record together and to this day, other than occasionally crossing paths on social media, the three have yet to again meet in person.

It was August 1985, a few weeks after Sari had told Charlie she didn't want to be with him anymore and that she had been seeing her Korean-American boss at the bank where she worked, that he was leaving his wife to marry her. Charlie went back to Chicago, devastated, and spent the next few months at home trying to pick up the pieces of his broken heart and make a new plan for the future which he wasn't sure would or would not include going back to Los Angeles.

One afternoon while Charlie was home alone at his parents' apartment, the phone rang. Not in any mood to answer the call and less inclined to talk to whoever was calling, he let the phone ring until the answering machine picked it up. It was Sari. She called to see how Charlie was doing after having heard reports from some of her old friends that he was sullen and depressed. She might have even been a little curious, if not jealous, to see if he had really started dating a former classmate of hers, which as it turned out he was, though it was more of a rebound thing than anything else. Hearing Sari's voice brought Charlie to tears and he decided to run over to the phone and pick it up just as she was finishing her message. They spoke for a few minutes, Charlie barely able to maintain his composure until Sari had to cut the call short as her boss/lover had come unannounced into her office at the bank where, thanks to her relationship with her boss, she was promoted to manager and a senior vice-president of one of the largest savings and loan associations in Southern California. After putting the phone back onto the receiver, Charlie sat down at his mother's 1946

Wurlitzer spinet and wrote the song that would become the foundation of a musical he planned to write about the hardships of relationships told through his experience of having lost Sari. In a single, one-hour sitting, the song was finished and Charlie had begun what would become his life's greatest ongoing challenge—one that would take him nearly forty years to bring to fruition. And it all started with a single, heart-wrenching love song…

Once upon a time
I was yours, you were mine
Nothing ever came between us;
Not secrets or lies
Oceans or skies
It was a love built on the sweetness in your eyes

Phone call, phone call from home
But it isn't my home anymore
Phone call, phone call from home
I should have fought for much more

Then the storm clouds blew in
And the rain and the wind
Washed our love far out to sea;
When the clouds went away
Our love had gone astray
The tempest is unforgiving that way

Phone call, phone call from home
But it isn't my home anymore
Phone call, phone call from home
I should have fought for much more

How many times
Must I rewrite these lines
Before you're back in my arms again
And when will this book
Take on a new look
And will these pages and hearts ever mend

Phone call, phone call from home
But it isn't my home anymore
Phone call, phone call from home
I should have fought for much more

It was that phone call from two thousand miles away and that song that would become the inspiration for the musical Charlie originally titled, *Great Big Town*. It was a fairly straightforward concept: boy meets girl, boy loses girl, girl realizes she gave up the love of her life and pleads for his forgiveness but he's already moved on and found the love of *his* life. Charlie wrote two more songs for the musical by the end of that summer: *Great Big Town* and *Best Years of My Life*. These were Charlie's interpretations of the kind of musical numbers you'd find in big Broadway shows sung by an actor and accompanied by a full stage of singers and dancers. Charlie loved musicals, especially those from the 1940s and 50s such as *Pal Joey*, *Carousel*, *West Side Story* and *The Pajama Game*. As a teen, Charlie played the role of Action in *West Side Story* in a local JCC production. It would be the last time he would act—or have anything to do with theater for more than twenty years. But more than any other musical, it was *Guys and Dolls* that opened on Broadway in 1950, that made Charlie fall in love with musical theater. When Charlie was about eleven or twelve, his cousin Linda belonged to a community theater company that put on *Guys and Dolls* in an East Rogers Park church hall. Linda played the role of Sister Sarah Brown and all that Charlie could remember from the show was the part where Sarah unknowingly gets inebriated by drinking rum and is kissed by the handsome gambler Sky Masterson. Charlie couldn't believe his eyes when he saw his own cousin being kissed on the lips before an audience full of people, making a big impression on the young Charlie. So much so, that the very next day he recreated the scene with his babysitter Marla, who was shocked when, out of the blue, Charlie planted a kiss directly on her lips while they were acting out what she thought was an innocent scene from a play Charlie had seen the night before. These musical stories stayed with Charlie his whole life, and while he never finished the musical, the ideas and songs remained a part of him and every few years he would dig up the notebook he had started that summer which, over the years, had become chock full of story ideas, song lyrics and page upon page of dialogue.

From his breakup with Sari in the summer of 1985 until some thirty-five years later, Charlie managed to live a whole life (some might say even more than one!). He did go back to Los Angeles in 1987, albeit briefly, to do that one final Café Society recording and tie up the loose ends of the five and a half years he had lived there. He was happy with the way the recording turned out and even considered staying to give the band another go, but there was something bigger, he thought, calling him to another place, so he returned to Chicago that summer. One day, Charlie received an invitation to attend a party at a friend's house—a girl he had met at a local poetry reading event with whom he had a short fling. At the party, Charlie was approached by a girl he had recognized but couldn't remember exactly from where. Ariane's mother worked with Charlie's mother in a Jewish gift shop and art gallery in Skokie, and when she walked over to say hello to Charlie who, at the last minute, remembered who she was, she gave him a big hug and two kisses on the cheek, immediately apologizing for the indiscretion, saying she had just returned from living in Spain for two years and was overly accustomed to greeting everyone that way. Charlie was intrigued by Ariane's travels and she was more than happy to talk about her experience. By the end of their conversation, Ariane had all but convinced Charlie to go to Spain, saying how much she thought he would love it and seeing how he was, as he put it, looking for a new adventure, Spain would provide all the allure and experiences he was looking for. Ariane agreed to meet Charlie one evening at the poetry café and came toting a little blue spiral notebook that she had filled with names, telephone numbers, restaurants, sites and attractions in Granada. That summer, Iberia Airlines began direct service from Chicago to Madrid, offering a great fare of five hundred dollars round trip with up to twelve months to return. He convinced his parents and grandparents to help him fund what was to be his first visit to Europe. His grandparents footed the bill for the flight and his parents pledged five-hundred dollars in cash, the idea being when the money ran out, Charlie would come home. What no one could have ever expected—not even Charlie himself— was that Charlie would fall in love with Spain, just like Ariane told him he would and just as she had.

Charlie arrived at Madrid's Barajas Airport early on the first Sunday morning in October 1987, armed with the blue notebook Ariane had given him which included, on the very first page, the telephone number of a small hotel owned by an older couple she had come to know on her travels to Madrid. Ariane had written to the couple to tell them a friend would be arriving in a few weeks and that he was reliable and trustworthy. Once Charlie's plane arrived and he collected his army-style duffle bag from the baggage carousel, he walked out into the empty airport to look for a public phone to call the hotel as Ariane had instructed him to do. But first, Charlie realized, he would need to change some dollars and get some coins for the phone. Walking around the airport, Charlie soon came to see that it was very early on a Sunday morning and that all the kiosks, cafés and *bureaus de change* were closed and from what he could gather, would open at eight a.m. Once they opened, Charlie was able to cash in some dollars and get a few coins for the phone. But that turned out to be the easy part. Around a corner, Charlie found a public telephone attached to a wall in a waiting area. He approached the phone and removed the odd assortment of coins he was given and as he proceeded to introduce the coins into the phone box, he soon realized he couldn't find a slot or any type of opening that would accommodate the insertion of coins; and in 1987 there were still a few years to go before phone cards were introduced. Charlie scanned the phone, up and down and all around, and there was nowhere for coins to go. Perhaps it was a special coinless phone for operator-assisted calls, he thought to himself, so he walked around the airport only to find every phone he came upon was the same, no slots, no slits and absolutely nowhere to put a coin. Frustrated and at the point of defeat, Charlie thought to ask one of the uniformed, patent leather tri-corner-hat-wearing civil guards if they would help him use the phone, but he was too embarrassed to ask and unsure if he would even be able to communicate. Just then, a woman walked up to the phone and placed a coin on the top of the phone box and, to his amazement, Charlie watched as the coin rolled down a narrow groove and dropped quickly out of sight into the box. *So, that was the secret*, Charlie said out loud to himself. He waited for the woman to finish her call and approached the phone placing, as he had seen the woman do, the coin atop the phone. After a few failed tries, he was finally able to get the coin into the groove and was delighted to hear it hit the bottom of the coin box which in turn sent a loud audible dial tone into his ear. He opened the blue notebook to the first page and dialed the number of the hotel that Ariane had written there and the phone began to ring in a peculiar tone he had never heard before. Then, it came. Someone answered. A voice that sounded as if it were from the beyond—an old man, Charlie thought. And then the voice spoke: *Dígame?* Charlie was speechless as he was unprepared for the man to answer the phone in Spanish. What now? Charlie thought to himself. Quickly, he remembered Ariane had written a few phrases for him in the blue notebook, but he was nervous thumbing through the pages while listening to *dígame? dígame!* coming from the telephone receiver. By the time he had come across the page with the phrases, the hotelkeeper had hung up the phone and Charlie decided the best solution would be to simply go to the hotel and try his luck communicating with the man in person. Luckily for Charlie, when he finally made it to the hotel, the man's wife answered the door, let him in and greeted him in near perfect English. *Now why couldn't she have answered the phone in the first place*, Charlie lamented under his breath.

Charlie spent a few days in Madrid before taking the train to his final destination and ended up staying in Granada for the better part of eighteen months, returning to Chicago in the spring of 1988 when he enrolled in a pilot playwriting program at The Theatre School of DePaul University, which boasted a rich history having been founded as the Goodman School of Drama in 1929. The school had a prestigious alumni list including Karl Malden, Sam Wanamaker, Geraldine Page, Shelley Berman, Harvey Korman, Linda Hunt, Joe Mantegna and, more recently, Gillian Anderson, who Charlie directed in a few short scenes during workshops at the end of every ten-week block. The following Christmas, during the school holidays, Charlie flew off to Granada to visit the many friends he had made during his time there, friendships he would maintain for a lifetime. On his first day back, he went around visiting his friends announcing his arrival and organizing dinner plans—at Gabriel's little off-the-grid pizzeria in the Campo de Principe. Popping into the Gimnasio Emperatriz, where his friend Saráh, a Moroccan Berber, worked, he found his friend on the phone yelling and gesticulating wildly. Saráh hung up the phone and greeted Charlie with a big hug and apologized for his rude interlude saying he was on the phone with the gym's aerobic teacher who called to say she wouldn't be coming to work that evening. Suddenly, Saráh came up with an idea and asked Charlie—who was the first male aerobics instructor in Granada during the time he lived there—if he would do the class as there were already a dozen or so girls waiting. Charlie said that not only had he not done aerobics since leaving Granada and was pretty out of shape, he didn't have the appropriate clothes on hand. "Not a problem," said Saráh, having remembered

Charlie left his old aerobics bag around the corner at Gimnasio Santa Mónica and that he could go and fetch it and come back in time for the class.

Charlie did his old friend a favor and led the aerobics class. After, Charlie showered and was heading out to go and drop his things off at his old friends Juan and Sally's place where he was staying before heading out to meeting everyone for dinner. As Charlie was walking out the door, he waved goodbye to Saráh who gestured for him to wait. Hanging up the phone, he walked around the other side of the counter and introduced Charlie to a young woman who was sitting alone in the reception area in a chair in the corner.

"This is Virginia," said Saráh. "She's a friend of mine and a student in my yoga class." I was just telling her about you and thought you two would get along."

Charlie was a bit taken by surprise and, not wanting to be rude despite being in a bit of a rush, sat down beside the young woman, who was shy and quite reserved, and said he would love to stay and talk, but had just arrived in town and needed to finish organizing a dinner party. He said if she didn't have any plans later, she was more than welcome to join in. She thanked Charlie for the invitation and he was off, though all the way to Juan and Sally's he couldn't stop thinking about his chance encounter with the young woman. There was something attractive about her that Charlie couldn't put his finger on. Perhaps it was the way she was dressed, which wasn't at all unlike the way Charlie was dressed, in ripped 501s and, even more to his surprise, black Dr. Marten's three-eyelet leather Oxfords, just like the ones he was wearing.

It turned out Virginia had a date that night but at the last minute she decided to back out, take up Charlie's dinner invitation and walk over to the Campo de Principe, where she found Charlie sitting at the head of a table with about seven or eight other guests. She walked in and Saráh immediately got up to greet his friend and, grabbing a free chair from the other end of the table, slid it in right beside Charlie. The first thing that Charlie discovered about Virginia was that, like himself, she had become a vegetarian about six months earlier. She had just finished university where she earned a degree in biology and was packing up her room getting ready for her father to drive down from Alicante to pick her up on Christmas Day. By the time dinner was over, Charlie was smitten and he could tell that Virginia felt the same way. He offered to walk her back to the apartment that she'd been sharing with some other girls from school which, coincidentally was in the same building on the Camino de Ronda (just up the street from Gimnasio Santa Mónica) where Charlie had rented a room for a short time when he first arrived in Granada. On the way back to Virginia's apartment, the two stopped off for chamomile tea at a swank bar called El Caballo Blanco, and stayed there until the wee hours of the morning when the manager kindly informed them he was about to close up. It was the week before Christmas and Charlie and Virginia spent every minute of every day together, walking around the city and delighting in the bright and beautiful ways Granada comes alive at Christmastime. They ate pizza at Gabriel's almost every night and had breakfast—usually *churros con chocolate*— in the Bib Rambla and even took an overnight trip up into the Alpujarra, where they observed the snow-capped mountains of the Sierra Nevada. On Christmas morning, Virginia accompanied Charlie on the two-hour bus ride to Malaga, where he was to catch a plane back home. On the

43

bus, Charlie, in a romantic but sincere gesture, gave Virginia the keys to his apartment and a twenty-dollar bill saying, "this will get you from the airport to my place and these will let you into my apartment. Just make sure to leave your shoes outside the door so I'll know you're there and won't get the daylights scared out of me!" That was Christmas Day. One month and a day later—the day of Virginia's twenty-fourth birthday—Charlie rented a car on a cold and blistery winter's day and drove to O'Hare Airport. There was Virginia, in her ripped 501s and Dr. Marten's, standing outside of the arrival's terminal with an oversized yellow plastic duffle. A year later, on April first (*Only fools get married*, Charlie would often say in jest), Charlie and Virginia walked into Chicago's City Hall and were married before a judge just before noon. With their marriage certificate in hand, Charlie went to the nearest pay telephone and called his mother to tell her the good news. While they were very much in love and did intend on marrying, they decided to expedite things when Virginia was offered a job doing research at the children's hospital where Charlie was doing his student teaching. The larger, more ceremonial wedding was held with their families and friends in attendance some four years later at the Heidel House Resort in Green Lake, Wisconsin, a place Charlie and Virginia had been going to and loved and said if they ever decided on a proper wedding, it would have to be there. And it was.

Charlie and Virginia stayed together for about fifteen years. They left Chicago in the summer of 1996 so that Virginia could finish her Ph.D. at the University of Valencia School of Medicine. They had two children—a son and a daughter—before divorcing in 2007. The two years following the divorce were perhaps the most difficult that Charlie had ever experienced and he drifted from job to job, house to house and from one relationship to another.

On his 44th birthday, he attended a party at the synagogue in Valencia and was introduced to a young woman, Natalia. Soon after, the couple started dating and fell deeply in love, but Natalia held a secret that would only be revealed later. She had been treated for schizophrenia and while the medications she'd been taking helped control her symptoms, they produced a wide range of secondary effects that she could no longer endure and told Charlie that she thought it would be best they end their relationship. After thinking long and hard about it, Charlie agreed, especially as he was uncertain how her behavior might impact his young son and daughter—who Natalia loved deeply. But a few months after he and Natalia parted ways, he felt that he could no longer live without her, that she was the love of his life and, no matter what the consequences, he would be there for her, care for her and do whatever was necessary to make their relationship work.

One hot Sunday morning, Charlie decided to get into his car and drive down to Alicante, to the village of San Juan, where Natalia had moved back in with her parents and younger sister. He pulled out in front of the house and called Natalia from the car, but there was no answer. He tried a few more times to no avail and just as he was about to get of the car and go over and knock on Natalia's door, his phone rang. How odd, he thought, as the phone number that appeared on the screen seemed to be out of the country and he didn't immediately recognize from where the call was coming. It was Natalia, who had seen that Charlie had been trying to call her for the past hour.

"I'm standing outside your parents' door," said Charlie, looking around to see if Natalia was walking around from the back of the house.

"I'm in Israel," Natalia said. "I arrived yesterday. I wanted to call you, but I didn't see any point."

Charlie was devastated and he hung up the call and drove back to Valencia in tears. A few years later he got up the nerve to reach out to Natalia's sister, Esther, who told him she was still in Israel, had finished her conversion and married an ultra-orthodox Jew, had a little girl and very little contact with her family though she seemed happy and well taken care of.

Alone, and facing the looming crisis that was about to wreak havoc on Spain's economy, Charlie prepared for the worst. In a short seven months he was forced to close the doors of his small neighborhood English school and liquidate the dozen bikes he used, just a year earlier, to pull billboard trailers by a team of cyclists who would ride the bikes all over the city promoting clients such as the city zoo, a local organic supermarket chain and a variety of small businesses.

It was in August of 2008 when Charlie joined Facebook, the popular up and coming social media platform that was all the craze at the time. It was there he re-connected with a former colleague, a Dutch woman with whom he worked at a private language school a few years earlier. It turned out she had been living in Japan with her Spanish husband when the two decided to part ways. Charlie mentioned, in a private message on the platform, that he too had recently divorced his Spanish spouse. And so it happened that she and Charlie got together one day at the end of August and took his kids and dogs down to the dry river bed for a picnic. The two talked about their future plans as they watched the children playing in the distance; she mentioned she had recently received a job offer from a university in Liverpool that she was seriously considering accepting. Charlie loved England and being a huge Beatles fan quipped that if she did indeed accept the job, he would join her. And that's just what happened.

They arrived in Liverpool in early January and settled into the Radisson Blu on Old Hall Street while they waited to take possession of a rented flat in the city center, just two blocks away from Mathew Street and the famous Cavern Club. Charlie was fighting a miserable head cold and tried to lift his spirits by eating the types of pleasure foods that weren't as readily available in Spain as they were in England. The two feasted on bagels, noodle soup cups, donuts and a wide variety of crisps and biscuits they would eat accompanied by cups of real English tea with milk.

They moved into their two-bedroom flat at number 1 Crosshall Street in Liverpool's L1 district, close to the Albert Docks and all the city center attractions. Eleven months later, their first daughter was born at Liverpool Women's Hospital, close to Penny Lane, and Charlie's kids came out that Christmas to meet their new baby sister and get their first taste of England, as well as their first snow storm.

In August 2010, they moved to the Netherlands, where Charlie became the designated stay-at-home parent, working two days a week teaching English at a hotel management school. In 2017, Charlie started his bow tie business and a year later, met Sam, thus starting Charlie's journey into the world of barbering. Soon after, Charlie's Night Barber concept took off and within a few months he'd be booked for sometimes a week or more in advance.

By the time the COVID-19 pandemic took hold in Europe, in March of 2020, Charlie was working three to four nights a week, earning more money than he ever did as a teacher and having the time of his life. Luckily for Charlie, the pandemic didn't have too much of a negative impact.

He rented a space for his barbershop at the back of a swank hair salon in one of The Hague's posher neighborhoods where one of his conditions for coming on board was that he only paid rent for the days he worked. Also, during the first long-term lockdown, Charlie received a modest compensation check from the local town council who had approved a generous scheme of helping small business owners during the closure. And it helped that the salary from her academic job covered most of the family's monthly expenses.

Charlie used the downtime to focus on some of his writing projects such as dusting off a few unfinished short stories and re-writing the novel he had written in 2011 which, while it was finished, he obsessed over, editing and re-writing the fifty-five-thousand-word novel over and over again with the idea of self-publishing it when he thought it was good enough to share with the world (or the dozen friends and family members who would most likely be the book's only readers). He also spent that spring watching a lot of films and series on Netflix. One film in particular, which he had heard about and was highly recommended by friends, was Noah Baumbach's 2019 film *Marriage Story* starring Adam Driver and Scarlett Johansson. While Charlie had never heard of Adam Driver he didn't make the connection to Driver and his small role in Steven Spielberg's 2012 historical drama *Lincoln* starring Daniel Day-Lewis as the title character, Abraham Lincoln. While Charlie had seen the film dozens of times and counted it among his favorite motion pictures of all time, he simply didn't remember seeing Driver in the film playing the part of telegraph operator Samuel Beckwith, which may have been easy to overlook as Driver had but only a few lines in the film.

Marriage Story made a huge impression on Charlie as it rekindled memories of his own divorce and challenges with child care and custody, though nothing as drastic or dramatic as were portrayed in the film. It also introduced him to Driver's immense talent, which Charlie was greatly impressed by. But it was one scene in the film that Charlie especially loved. Driver's character who, interestingly enough, was named Charlie Barber, was out with some members of his New York City-based theater company for drinks at a local lounge. Suddenly, Driver stood up and began singing *Being Alive*, from Stephen Sondheim's 1970 Tony Award-winning musical *Company*, which the lounge pianist happened to be playing at the time. Watching Driver singing that song immediately brought Charlie (our Charlie) to tears. Uncontrollable tears. It was at that very moment when our Charlie made a connection to *that* Charlie, a connection that would go far beyond anything he could have ever imagined. Over the next few weeks, Charlie watched *Marriage Story* a few more times, focusing deeper and deeper on Driver's performance, thinking there was something more to the actor than he had initially thought that went far and beyond his astute ability and dedication to his craft. No, Charlie thought to himself, there was something more. Much more.

Towards the end of March, Charlie realized he hadn't spoken to his son in Valencia since the beginning of the pandemic, too worried about the uncertainties of the disease and confused and frightened by all the conflicting news reports that were bombarding the 24-hour news cycle and social media outlets. And he was right for being concerned as he fell into the category of individuals who were considered high risk—over fifty and asthmatic—for acquiring this, at the time, little understood disease.

Charlie and his son were close, as close as any father and son could be and spoke almost daily. But by the end of March, it appeared his son wanted no part of his father and Charlie, being Charlie, didn't want to press the issue and was hurt to the point of not being able to reach out to his son for fear of rejection. And that's what it was. His son. Adam Driver reminded Charlie of his son. Something about their physical resemblance. Something about their soft-spoken gentleness. Charlie connected to Adam Driver because he reminded Charlie of his son.

In May, Charlie decided to buy a new digital piano for two of his daughters who had expressed an interest in taking lessons to while away their time during the pandemic and frequent lockdowns and school closures. Once the piano was delivered, Charlie became reacquainted with playing and dug out his old notebook of lyrics and story ideas for the musical he had started writing all those years ago. But this time was different. More than just a short drive down memory lane, Charlie was inspired to dig a little deeper, explore the possibilities a bit further, and seeing how he was so filled with inspiration, he thought this might be the moment he'd been waiting for all these years; maybe this was the right time to re-visit writing the musical, but in earnest, with intention and clarity.

Over the summer, Charlie sat at the piano every day playing his songs, working on some new ones and pondering how to get started on revamping his decades-old project. He loved the songs, found them still relevant and poignant—and loved singing them. But there had been so many ever-changing storylines over the years that he couldn't even begin to make sense or conjure up a story that would tie all the songs together. He realized the lyrics could always be re-tooled to fit any motif, but the songs—especially the original three he wrote in August 1985—would be difficult to modify. He didn't want to change them as he feared losing the initial creative spark that ignited the flame of his desire to write a musical in the first place. Towards the end of the summer, Charlie was growing more and more keen to explore new possibilities and began to think long and hard about what he could write about that would make an interesting storyline for his musical. He found the answer he was looking for when he started exploring a bit further into the career of Adam Driver after having a visit from a new customer on September 20th.

Charlie's first customer that warm September evening was a first-timer named Michael, a Dutchman who Charlie thought to be in his early thirties and who—to Charlie's amazement—had an uncanny resemblance to, of all people, Adam Driver. Michael was tall and lanky, but athletic and handsome in an untypical and indescribable way, like Adam Driver was. At least that's how Charlie thought about it. His height, facial composition, body type, even the hair—especially the hair!—was Adam Driver. And Michael was reserved, soft-spoken and genteel (just like Charlie imagined the real Adam Driver might be). Charlie went home that evening after his shift at the barbershop and started watching trailers of Adam Driver films on YouTube and came across one that immediately caught his attention, and for a reason that was nostalgically pleasing to Charlie. In that particular film, Adam Driver plays a bus driver who, in his free time, writes poetry. How divine, Charlie thought to himself remembering his childhood dream of becoming a bus driver. He would spend hours playing bus at his grandparents' house, taking a round corduroy pillow from the couch and setting it atop his grandmother's sideboard, where the family's Passover dishes and imported bottles of Israeli liqueur were stored. Charlie would sit on the small red vinyl chair the downstairs neighbor Kurt Hoffman gave him and he would meticulously set out his transfer slips (that everyone in the family would save from their public transport journeys), hole puncher (to validate the transfers, of course) and a tidy stack of timetables from the number 84 Peterson Avenue bus line that ran near his house to the Bryn Mawr 'L' station.

In the film *Paterson* (close enough to Peterson, thought Charlie) released in 2016 (the year Charlie's beloved Chicago Cubs won their first World Series pennant in 108 years) and directed by Jim Jarmusch, Driver plays a bus driver named Paterson (*My real name is Paterson*, he replies when asked by another of the film's characters). Paterson, who was born, lives and drives a bus in, of all places, Paterson, New Jersey, writes poems styled after his favorite poet William Carlos Williams, who was a physician born in nearby Rutherford, New Jersey. He spent most of his life and died there in March of 1963, 108 days (see Cubs reference above!) before Charlie was born at Louis A. Weiss Memorial Hospital on Marine Drive in Chicago, Illinois. In the film, Paterson lives with his wife Laura, beautifully played by the beautiful Iranian-French actress Golshifteh Farahani, and their English bulldog

Marvin (who was actually played by a female dog named Nellie, who sadly died shortly after the film was made and became the first dog ever to win a posthumous Palm Dog award at the Cannes Film Festival in 2016). Paterson drives the number 23 bus through Paterson, New Jersey. Coincidentally (if you believe in such occurrences), the number 23 bus, operated by the Dutch public transport operator HTM, is the bus line that runs through the town of Rijswijk, where Charlie and his family have lived just outside of The Hague since 2011. There's rarely a day that goes by when Charlie doesn't see the number 23 bus rolling through his neighborhood.

A few important things happened the first time Charlie watched *Paterson*. First, he discovered in that 118-minute film one of the best films he'd ever seen, which was actually problematic for someone who studied playwriting, dialogue, directing, acting and who was, to say the least, a cinephile. The problem? Well, while the film was very well executed, the cinematography and editing, by Frederick Elmes and Alfonso Gonçalves respectively, flawless and ever so slightly edgy; Jarmusch's vision, brilliant; and the lead performances played so authentically, exquisite; there was no plot, no conflict (per se), no high drama or hijinks, no death or destruction, explosions, violence (well…you couldn't really call the "gun scene" *violence*), no suspense, no intrigue and only three swear words.

Second, Charlie felt a connection to Adam Driver on a few different levels: the bus driver thing, of course, and the poetry thing. As it turns out, Charlie has been writing poems since Mrs. English's fourth grade class at De Witt Clinton Elementary School, when she would send him out of the classroom for one of the many infractions he would commit: crawling on the sleek polished hardwood floors, passing notes, taunting Betty Ann McCracken, talking and—what drove Marcia English crazier than anything—Charlie's filling his notebooks with lines and verses and stanzas of poetry, short stories, skits and stick figure cartoons). But finally, it was his shared admiration for the poet William Carlos Williams. But it was when William Carlos Williams was revealed as an underlying, recurring theme of the film, Charlie noticed a peculiar inconsistency which had him perplexed and turning to the internet for answers. As it turns out, Charlie had been writing poems for almost forever. And when Charlie wasn't writing poetry, he was reading poetry and had an insatiable appetite for poems. And William Carlos Williams—along with Sylvia Plath, e.e. cummings, Robert Frost, Louise Glück, Allen Ginsburg, Emily Dickinson and Li-Young Lee—was amongst his favorites. But it was the work of William Carlos Williams—especially his 1944 book *The Wedge*, a collection of poems he assembled in a small pocket-sized book that U.S. servicemen could take with them to the war—that Charlie chose to write a graduate school paper on for Richard Jones' class, arguing the book was, as Charlie wrote, "as important to the soldier as a rifle or bayonet that, while those could save their lives, poetry would save their souls."

Charlie watched *Paterson* with keen interest and an astute eye for detail, but it wasn't until after he watched the film for the second time that summer evening that it hit him. The film makes countless references to Williams having lived and practiced medicine in Paterson, when in fact, he lived and worked in nearby Rutherford. So, Charlie took to the internet again to see what he could find and confirm what he knew to be true, that Williams was born and died in Rutherford. On Charlie's second viewing of the film, he came to a scene early on when Adam Driver is sitting at Doc's bar looking around observing the unextraordinary goings on—two men playing chess, a woman making a selection at the juke box—when his attention turned to the wall behind the bar where Doc had taped a variety of Paterson-themed photos, newspaper clippings and whathaveyou when the camera stops on a business card taped to the wall that, in addition to a phone number in the top right corner and office hours in the bottom left read:

William Carlos Williams, M.D.
131 W. Passaic Avenue
Paterson, N.J.

That caught Charlie's attention and immediately he felt somewhat perplexed. So, he paused the film, closed the movie viewer window and started asking Google a million questions until he not only found the answer he was looking for, he found the exact same business card on a website that had the exact same information in the exact same layout on the exact same white business card, exactly the same except for one minor detail; instead of Paterson, N.J. printed at the bottom of the card, the city was printed as Rutherford, N.J. But maybe I'll leave that part of the story for later and get back to Charlie's story.

Now, I'm not trying to suggest that Charlie was becoming obsessed with Adam Driver, it wasn't like that at all, though he did talk quite at length about the actor, his films and the roles he played (call it a man crush if you must!). What I think, and it's just a personal observation, is that Adam Driver—and even his new customer Michael, who reminded Charlie of Adam Driver—*both* reminded Charlie of his son who, by now, he hadn't spoken to in well over a year. The next time I saw Charlie, he was somewhat frenzied and anxious and I knew something was definitely up.

Ten days after Michael had come into the shop for the first time, he booked another appointment, but this time it was for his two young sons. When Michael arrived with his boys, Charlie was happy to see him again and was overcome by a feeling he was being visited by a spirit, that maybe it was a message from some alternative universe beckoning Charlie to open his eyes and take a good long look at what was going on around him…and inside of him. There before him stood a likeness of both the actor he had come to know and admire and the son with whom he had become estranged.

After work that night, Charlie came home, made himself two peanut butter and jelly sandwiches, chips and a hot mug of tea and sat down to watch the Cubs play one of their last games of the season, obliterating the Pittsburgh Pirates in a nine-to-nothing shutout to win the three-game series. By the time the game ended, it was already near morning and Charlie was ready for bed. But just as he was about to shut off the TV, he saw the preview image of the film *Paterson* on the screen and selected it. The movie, which he had been watching a few days earlier, started somewhere in the middle, a scene where the camera is focusing on Driver as he drives along the busy streets of Paterson (the actor actually learned how to drive a real bus for the film). The camera pans from close-ups of Driver to shots out of the bus's front, side and door windows, capturing everyday scenes of traffic, pedestrians and people walking in and out of shops along the city's bustling main streets. Just then, Charlie got lost in a daydream (and a real daydream at that as by now the sun was just starting to rise and set the sky outside of Charlie's living room window aglow). What if, he thought to himself, he had become a bus driver. He imagined one day driving a bus in Chicago, perhaps the number 147 Outer Drive Express, whose north-south route began at the Howard Street 'L' station then, some thirty stops later, at Foster Avenue and Marine Drive (about 900 feet or three blocks away from the hospital where Charlie was born), jumps onto the Outer Drive and goes express to Michigan Avenue and Delaware Place. Then, three stops later at Michigan and Erie a familiar looking fellow boards the bus and greets Charlie with a pleasant smile. He recognizes the passenger because it's the famous actor, Adam Driver. How interesting, Charlie thought to himself, this famous actor boards his bus on Michigan and Erie, just steps away from the Crate & Barrel, which closed in 2018 to be replaced by Starbuck's Coffee, whose massive four-story café, retail shop and roastery would become the company's largest outlet in the world, opening its doors in 2019 after a ten-million-dollar renovation. And why did Charlie find that so interesting, poignant even? It was at that very location where once stood Chandler's French Room Shoes, an upscale women's shoe store where Charlie's grandfather worked for more than forty years and where Charlie, as a boy, would occasionally spend a Saturday or school holiday as his grandfather's right-hand man, helping him pull shoes from the wall stock or running upstairs to the dimly lit storeroom where, what seemed to Charlie like a million boxes filled with pantyhose, shoe polish, handbags and other accessories, were stored. Charlie's favorite part of the day was having lunch at the swanky Churchill's a few doors down where Charlie and his grandfather would sit at the counter on tufted swivel chairs and eat cheeseburgers with steak fries and chocolate malts. Churchill's was owned by Charlie's classmate Arthur Balourdos's father and uncle. The two Greek immigrants came to the United States in 1957, opening a string of popular restaurants including Steven's on Wacker, visited regularly by Illinois governor Jim Thompson and many Chicago politicians and city elites. Sadly, Arthur's father Michael died at the age of sixty-six in 1996, just as his commercial real estate business was starting to boom, a business that today Arthur and his family own and operate, having made the humble family of immigrants wealthy in one of the many American Dream stories you often hear about. That's where Charlie's daydream ended and the exact moment an idea was born.

By early fall, Charlie had gone from watching *Paterson* every few days to putting it on the iPad he used to listen to movies at night as they helped him fall asleep (*better than sleeping pills*, Charlie would tell himself). He'd been doing it for years, first with *Shawshank*, then *Lincoln* (where Adam Driver had his small role), then *Pal Joey*, the 1957 Hollywood adaptation of the Rodgers and Hart musical starring Rita Hayworth, Frank Sinatra and Kim Novak, which was by far and away Charlie's favorite big screen musical. After that, Charlie would be quickly lulled to sleep by Robert Duvall and Robert Downey, Jr.'s 2014 film, *The Judge*, Pedro Almodovar's *Dolor y Gloria* (which was Charlie's first Spanish-language sleepytime film); *Moneyball* (his longest lasting nighttime film up to that point that had put him to sleep for nearly an entire year); and finally, the film that would outlast even *Moneyball*, *Paterson*, which remained Charlie's ticket to dreamland for two years, seven months and, well, more days than he could remember. The more Charlie would think about *Paterson*, the more he became enthralled by exactly what it was about this simple film that had him so totally absorbed in it. After all, it was a film that, for seven days, followed the life and times of a guy who drove a bus and wrote poems and who was married to a homemaker who spent her days doing DIY projects, baking cupcakes and dreaming about becoming a country singer. But it was Charlie's innate curiosity and unconventionally quixotic imagination that wasn't satisfied with how the film ended. Normally, Charlie would see a film and when *The End* flashed upon the screen and the closing credits rolled, that would be it, end of story and Charlie would either give his thumb up or thumb down and move on. But something different happened at the end of *Paterson*, something that left Charlie unsettled and questioning. He simply wanted more. Charlie carried on working on his showtunes and mulling over ideas about how he could develop a story that would become his new musical, one that would rise from the proverbial ashes of long-departed ideas and take the form of something real, something that, Charlie thought, could be worthy of even Broadway.

And it came to be that in early December, Michael came back for another haircut. That was all it took to set Charlie's imagination ablaze. As he cut Michael's hair—albeit in a much shorter version of what Adam Driver's hair looked like in the films Charlie had been watching lately (*Annette, The Report, BlacKkKlansman, This is Where I Leave You* and *Frances Ha*)—he was overcome by the strangest notion. What would he do if Adam Driver came into his shop one evening for a haircut? What would that be like, to cut the hair of a famous movie star, and not just *any* famous movie star, *his* favorite famous movie star. Charlie mulled that over for a few minutes, concluding that he knew exactly what he would say.

CHAPTER TWO

THE SEQUEL

Charlie grew more and more preoccupied with *Paterson*, his mind racing with ideas about how he imagined the story of Paterson and Laura might continue. One day, he sat down in front of his computer and just started to write, and what he had written after about thirty minutes of hunting and pecking on his keyboard was a short film treatment, the detailed overview one writes as a summary of a proposed film or screenplay.

After finishing the treatment, Charlie stared intensely, and proudly, at the computer screen thinking long and hard about a title for his screenplay, but he couldn't come up with anything he really liked, so he settled on the obvious: *A Return to Paterson*. The idea was simply to continue Jim Jarmusch's story, answering Charlie's question: *what happens next?* He had a million possible answers and outlined the most compelling ones in his film treatment. Paterson and Laura would split up, Laura's desire to have children—and twins, at that (a recurring theme of the original film)—was just too daunting for Paterson, who worried about the expenses of raising a child (or two) and bringing children into an uncertain world that seemed to be more topsy-turvy than anything else. He also wanted to spend more time writing poetry, especially after the series of incidents that occurred at the end of the film. In Charlie's film, the couple go their separate ways. Charlie becomes the first new poet laureate of New Jersey (which was officially known as the *New Jersey William Carlos Williams Certificate of Merit*) since the post was re-established by Governor Chris Christie in 2010. It had earlier been abolished when the state General Assembly voted 69 to 2 in favor of the bill to rescind it which was signed by then Governor James E. McGreevey on July 2, 2003. The following year, Paterson is appointed poet laureate of the United States, replacing Louise Glück, and moves from the house he had lived in his entire life to a small studio apartment in Forestville, Maryland, just outside of D.C.

In Charlie's film treatment, Laura follows her dream of becoming a country star and moves to Nashville, where she rents a small apartment owned by her father's cousin, who moved to Nashville from Iran with her family in the 1970s and taught paralegal studies at Nashville State College. One night while performing at an open mic at the Bluebird Café in Green Hills, her talent piques the interest of a record company scout who was in the audience. After her set, the scout approaches Laura backstage and offers to put her in the studio to make a demo. In just three short months, Laura signs a six-figure record deal and releases her first single, one she co-wrote with Matraca Berg and her husband, Jeff Hanna, known for being a member of the Nitty Gritty Dirt Band.

Laura's music career took off and she soon saw another one of her dreams come true. A group of investors including Michael Tattersfield, President and CEO of Krispy Kreme Doughnuts, launched her Cupcake Queen cupcake company, selling her trademark black and white cupcakes at each and every one of Krispy Kreme's nearly thousand global stores. In addition to that, Laura opened her flagship Cupcake Queen at 310 Broadway in Nashville, opposite Jason Aldean's restaurant and bar. Laura also sold her own home décor line, designer clothing collections and to top it all off she opened Marvin's, a dog café and *barkery* (as she called it) in the far back corner of the shop.

Charlie had devised the story he wanted to tell, well, at least he had come up with a story he would want to see made into the sequel of his (now) favorite film. So, what was next? Having earned a bachelor of fine arts degree in playwriting, Charlie knew how to craft a good story and write dialogue, but the work of the playwright and that of the screenwriter differ in a few fundamental ways. Playwrights focus on crafting scripts for live performances on stage, using dialogue and minimal stage directions to convey the essence of the story within the immediate interaction of a live audience. In contrast, screenwriters create scripts for film or television, employing a detailed screenplay format that includes visual descriptions, camera directions and a variety of collaborative elements to guide the production team in translating the narrative into a visual medium. Charlie got the gist of it, but felt intimidated by the process, so he turned to the internet and began the tedious work of teaching himself how to write a screenplay. The first thing Charlie did was buy a yearlong subscription to MasterClass, an online education platform where world-renowned experts teach classes from everything to art and entertainment to cooking, science and writing. His first class was dramatic writing, taught by Pulitzer Prize-winning playwright, author and filmmaker David Mamet. Mamet, who grew up on Chicago's South Shore, moved to the North Side as a teenager where his mother would shop at the Jewel food store where Charlie's mother worked as a checker with a man who was the assistant manager who she would marry in 1970, adopting Charlie a year later. Charlie's mother would often re-tell the story of how Mamet's mother would come into the supermarket bragging about her son the playwright saying, "My son David's going off to become famous in New York City." It took some time, but bragging rights were definitely in the stars for Lenore Mamet. And her now-famous son. After completing Mamet's online master class, Charlie moved on to screenwriting by Aaron Sorkin, filmmaking by Martin Scorsese and David Lynch and directing by Ron Howard and Spike Lee. What Charlie learned from these *masters* in their master classes gave him the knowledge he was seeking—and the confidence he needed—to sit down at the computer and begin working on his screenplay in earnest.

In about six weeks, Charlie had finished what he felt was a decent first draft of his screenplay *A Return to Paterson*. In fact, Charlie was downright ecstatic. Four weeks later, the Dutch government called for another total lockdown and curfew to battle the newest wave of the pandemic, so Charlie found himself with some extra time which he used to go through his screenplay with an editor's eye and fine-tooth comb. And before he returned to the barbershop, he felt his screenplay was polished and worthy of other eyes to read. But what other eyes and how he would get his screenplay in front of those eyes were two important questions Charlie had to answer. Charlie figured he'd go straight to the source and send his treatment with a few sample pages to *Paterson* director Jim Jarmusch. Once again, he turned to Google and went straight for the kill: *How do I contact Jim Jarmusch?* he typed into the search engine, only to get back over three million hits, many of which were seemingly reputable websites, like Variety and IMDB, but all required some form of paid subscription to access their information. He found Jarmusch had verified accounts on Instagram and Twitter, and while he followed him on those accounts, there would be little to no chance of ever engaging with him on those platforms. *What next*? he asked himself. Thinking long and hard, and trying to be resourceful, Charlie remembered his childhood pediatrician, the late Dr. Benjamin Emanuel (with whom Charlie reconnected years later as they both worked at the children's hospital and would occasionally meet for coffee and cake in the hospital's cafeteria). Dr. Ben had three sons: one none other than Rahm, the former mayor of Chicago; another, the world-renowned oncologist and bioethicist Zeke (who formed part of President Biden's COVID-19 Advisory Board) and finally, and most relevant to the story, Ari, the Hollywood super-agent and CEO of Endeavor, one of the most important and influential entertainment and media companies in the world. If only Charlie could find a way to reach out to Ari, he thought, and a good thought it was. After all, there was certainly a connection. Finding a way to contact Ari Emanuel was actually easier than Charlie could have imagined. He found the telephone number of Endeavor's Beverly Hills headquarters right on their corporate website, picked up the phone and dialed. He told the receptionist he'd like to speak with Ari Emanuel, that he was former patient, colleague and family friend of his late father's, which wasn't a big stretch from the truth as both Ari's father Dr. Ben, and his wife Marsha, were longtime customers at Charlie's mother's Jewish gift shop in suburban Chicago. The receptionist was quick to say that most of Ari's friends had his personal phone number and she advised Charlie that would be the best way to get a hold of him. *Of course*, Charlie said, thanking the receptionist and hanging up the phone feeling the sting of stupidity. Returning to the Endeavor website and jotting down its Wilshire Boulevard address, Charlie opened a blank Word document and began a long, very personal letter to Ari Emanuel, which he then printed and included in an envelope with a copy of the treatment and first five pages of his screenplay. The letter was never acknowledged, not even with a *Dear Sir* form letter.

In the weeks and months that followed, Charlie would send letters and emails to just about everyone connected to *Paterson* he could find, including the producers, executive producers, cinematographer, casting and second unit personnel—just about anyone and everyone from the full cast and crew list on the IMDB Charlie thought might be a champion for getting him in touch with Jim Jarmusch. And the result from that massively time-consuming undertaking was not as much as a tug on the line. No biting fish and no way of getting to Jim Jarmusch.

As time went by, Charlie grew more and more confident that his *Paterson* sequel idea was a good one, if not a great one, and he wasn't going to let the defeats of the past put a damper on his efforts for the future. He needed a new plan and maybe the key to that plan had been staring him in the face all along. And who'd been staring at him all along was Adam Driver.

By now, Charlie knew as much about Driver as anyone—maybe even as much as the actor knew about himself and his career. After marrying his longtime girlfriend Joanne Tucker, who he met during their time as students at New York's Julliard School, the couple settled in the New York's Brooklyn Heights neighborhood, with its charming brownstones and tree-lined streets and picturesque views of the East River. Charlie knew that Driver was as un-Hollywood as movie stars come, as his choice of choosing to live in New York over L.A. attested. And Driver, despite being a huge Hollywood star thanks to the global stardom his role as Kylo Ren from the *Star Wars* franchise brought him, he was, deep down, a thespian whose love, respect and admiration for the theater was marrow deep. It finally hit Charlie that the only way to get his screenplay made into a film would be to get it into the hands of the actor who played the title role, and if he could get Adam Driver on board, surely the movie star could convince Jarmusch and his co-stars to come on board as well for the sequel. Charlie, though he didn't really know it at the time, had just conceived his master plan 2.0. While he was satisfied with his screenplay, he still felt far removed from the whole idea of making movies. He understood that if and when his screenplay would be optioned, the real pros would take over and his idea would be made into a cinema-worthy film. But that would be the tip of a very large iceberg and take years—if ever—to make. Charlie needed to regroup and I'm delighted to say that I played a part—albeit a small part— in the next stage (no pun intended) of Charlie's story.

I booked in for a haircut at my now usual last appointment slot on a Monday night. Mentioning my appreciation for Charlie's choice of business plan and the after-hours aspect of what was typically a nine-to-five business, he said it worked out well in getting him off the hook for being home in the evenings a few nights a week, especially between dinner and bedtime. Apparently, that's when pandemonium rang out at Charlie's house where his three school-age daughters fussed over dinner, homework, iPhones, showers and settling down for bedtime. At the end of the day, whether Charlie thought he was a good barber or not, he was, after all, the *only* barber in town who'd cut your hair and trim your beard on a Monday night (or any night) at eleven p.m. (I've said it before and it's worth repeating!).

On this particular Monday night, Charlie was in an especially enlivened frame of mind, talkative (more than usual), animated (also more than usual) and noticeably more distracted. He went on to confess that he had come up with an idea and wanted to run it by me. He explained the whole Adam Driver story, about his customer Michael (the Adam Driver doppelganger who was really the inspiration behind getting the train rolling) and the plan about writing a sequel to an Adam Driver film. And while I hadn't seen any of his films up until that point, I had of course heard of his portraying Kilo Ren in *Star Wars,* as you basically had to live in another universe to have *not* heard about role made famous by Driver. Charlie told me he had seen Driver in a film and was so taken by the film that he actually wrote a screenplay for the sequel (which I thought was a little over the top, even for Charlie, who could be a little over the top at times). So, he wrote this screenplay and had been trying to get it out there to no avail. His new idea, which he confessed was pretty far out there, was to write a three-part musical for the stage based on his film sequel idea. At least that's how I first understood it. But it would be split up into three very different parts, he explained. The first part would be a one-man show, where he would explain the whole Adam Driver story, interlaced with the story of how, in August of 1985, he began writing a musical inspired by his breakup with an old girlfriend. Now here's the kicker. The entire one-man show would be Charlie on stage in a make-believe barbershop, playing the part of a barber who was a retired teacher who studied playwrighting, moved to Spain, got married—well, you see where the thing was going. And during the seventy-minute show, Charlie would be telling his stories interspersed with five or six musical numbers with a *real* customer sitting in a *real* barber chair and, get this, getting a *real* haircut while Charlie tells his stories and sings. At first, I didn't really know how to react or to respond to what Charlie had just told me, but he said it with such zeal and commitment to what he thought was a truly great and novel idea, that his infectious enthusiasm rubbed off on me and I told him that not only did I love the idea, but that I'd be the first person to buy a front-row ticket to the Broadway premiere. Charlie went on to explain the rest of the concept, and as he delved deeper and deeper, I was drawn equally as deep into the journey with him.

In the end, the idea was to write the one-man musical as a sort of prelude, something he could use to measure the level of interest there may or may not be for such a show. If the one-man show worked, he continued, the second part of the trilogy would be a full-blown, Broadway-style musical—big cast, chorus line, more musical numbers, costumes, sets, orchestra—the whole shebang. This would be a musical that, in the first act, would be a review of the first part—the one-man show—only bigger and better. Act two would show Charlie taking his musical to New York, spending every penny of his life's savings to mount the production at an off-off-Broadway theater where he would lure the real Adam Driver to see a performance, and once he coaxed him onto the stage and into his barber's chair, he would pitch Driver the idea of the sequel and—as if that wasn't already a lofty enough plan—convince Driver to not only star in the sequel, but to reunite the entire cast and crew to be a part of it and—as the icing on the cake—persuade Driver to put up a million dollars of his own capital and invest in the film as an executive producer.

Charlie titled his extravaganza *Adam Driver and the Million Dollar Haircut*. Now if that ain't one hell of a title, I thought to myself. I mean, it sounded great when it burst out of Charlie's mouth, sounding like it could actually *be* a Broadway musical. I could actually envision seeing that on a marquee, maybe at the Gershwin or the Majestic or the Barrymore. But there was a third part to the story and Charlie was revved up to tell me about it. The final part of the musical would be (wait until you hear this) the sequel to the movie *Paterson*. Not as a movie, but as…you guessed it…as another musical!

Charlie was whipped up into a frenzy as he explained the third and final part of his musical trilogy, *A Return to Paterson*, going over the story point by point: the breakup of Paterson and Laura, their each moving to new cities to explore their new careers and then, going back to his original 1985 themes of breakups and reunions, Charlie, at the end of the play, has the couple getting back together and taking the stage in a scene set at Doc's bar Shades. There, the couple arrive pushing a double-buggy (twins, we imagine). They are greeted by Doc and his wife, Donny (Paterson's former supervisor from the bus depot) and Everett and Marie, the couple from the first film whose tempestuous relationship was a sub-plot and who now are happily married, with Marie visibly pregnant. And just as celebrations are getting underway, the Japanese poet Paterson encounters at the Great Falls of the Passaic River near the end of the film walks into the bar and is heartily greeted by Paterson, who segues into the play's final musical number. Just as the number is coming to its close, Paterson and Laura's dog Marvin runs out onto the stage and is picked up by Paterson and embraced by the couple. The song ends and the Japanese poet approaches Paterson, hands him a blank notebook and says his most iconic line from the film: "Sometimes [an] empty page presents most possibilities." And as Paterson takes the notebook, the Japanese poet turns, walks to the door, stops and turns around saying (as he did while exiting his scene in the film): "Excuse me…A-ha!" And just then, the entire cast stops what they're doing, looks at the Japanese poet and, in unison, chants: "A-ha!" The curtain falls and the play has ended.

CHAPTER THREE

A ONE-MAN SHOW

C harlie now had his work cut out for him with clear direction and razor-sharp focus. The first thing he needed to do was to find a pianist to transcribe the songs (Charlie never learned to read or write music) and accompany him during rehearsals and, when the time was right, performances. Next, Charlie needed a venue and while there were many small cabaret-style theaters in The Hague—and other Dutch cities he envisioned taking his show to—he thought it best to start out small and what better, smaller place than his own barbershop?

Charlie met with the owner of the hair salon where, at the back of the shop, he rented a custom-made barber corner. Charlie told him about his project and asked permission to use the salon one or two Saturday nights to test out his new play. The idea was to invite a dozen of his oldest, most trusted customers to see the show, enjoy some wine and cheese and discuss the performance. To his delight, the owner gave Charlie permission—and his blessings—to use the salon for the show. One day, while scrolling though posts on a local expat Facebook group, Charlie came across a post by a Ukrainian pianist who lived in the next village and was advertising for students. Charlie sent the pianist a message asking if he might be interested in transcribing a few songs and the man agreed and the two set a price. Charlie sent the man a recording of the musical's opening number he had recorded on his iPhone and sent it, along with the lyrics, to the man who, a few days later came over to Charlie's house and played him the song. Charlie was totally blown away as this was the first and only time he had ever heard anyone playing one of his own songs. He was so overcome with emotion that he could barely sing the opening line of the song once Henny, the Ukrainian pianist, sat down, began playing and nodded for Charlie to start singing. That was the beginning of a mutually beneficial relationship in that Henny came on board as Charlie's arranger and accompanist and Charlie took on the role of Henny's manager, arranging performances, tours and master classes around Europe for Henny, who had only six months earlier arrived in the Netherlands after leaving his war-torn country and joining his wife and young daughter—also concert pianists—abroad. Now, Charlie needed to find a director and there was only one person for the job.

Charlie met Abbott Chrisman in early 1989 after enrolling in the playwriting program at The Theatre School of DePaul University. Abbott, who had graduated from the renowned theater conservatory's Master of Fine Arts in Directing program a year earlier, was hired to teach, among other things, a freshman course called History of Dramatic Literature that Charlie had signed up for. When Charlie graduated with a degree in playwriting, he decided to stay on at DePaul and do a combined master's degree in History and English, and when it came time for Charlie to publish the book of poetry he wrote for his thesis project, he reached out to Abbott, who by then had moved to Zurich, Switzerland and was teaching at Webster University in Geneva (making the two hour and forty-three minute train commute two to three times a week). Abbott, who had kept in touch with Charlie by sending him his annual family advent letter (complete with drawings by Abbott's two, then young, daughters), was thrilled to hear from him and agreed to be an advisor on his final project. The two kept in touch over the years, exchanging letters, then emails and, when Charlie moved to the Netherlands in 2010, they saw each other from time to time, in Geneva, on a family trip once and then twice in the Netherlands, where Abbott had come to attend work-related conferences and to see his old friend and former student. Charlie wrote to Abbott with a long-winded, detailed email of what he was working on and opened the letter with: *Dear Abbott, I'm writing to congratulate you on being selected as the director for the new Broadway-bound musical, 'Adam Driver and the Million Dollar Haircut'.* The next day, Abbott responded to Charlie's email by writing: *I'd be absolutely delighted to be your co-pilot on this adventure; let's talk soon.*

Over the next few months, Charlie began rehearsals with Henny and maintaining weekly Monday morning video chats with Abbott, keeping him abreast of how things were moving along. In February, Abbott flew to The Hague and spent a week working with Charlie and Henny at a music rehearsal studio near Charlie's house. Every morning for seven days, the three men met at the studio at nine a.m., had coffee and donuts that Henny would pick up on his way and worked on putting the show together. By the end of the week, everything seemed to just meld and Charlie was ecstatic, confident and ready to take the next step and present his show to the world, well, at least to the first dozen customers he planned on inviting to see the show at the barbershop.

I remember that evening so vividly. It was early April and it seemed that spring had come early to the Netherlands as it was a beautiful, warm and slightly windy evening; daylight savings time had recently started and there was still a bit of sunlight glowing in the evening sky. I arrived at seven-thirty as I told Charlie I'd show up early and be around if he needed anything, which of course he did and I was delegated to set up the refreshments table at the back of the shop in the waiting room. Charlie had overdone it, as I imagined was his nature. There were bottles of expensive Spanish Rioja and German Riesling, which I was instructed to put on ice; there was bourbon and Scotch and two types of tequila (I cut limes and had to run over to the supermarket for a small box of salt, which Charlie had overlooked). At about eight-fifteen, the first of Charlie's eleven other customers began to arrive. For me, this was already starting to be an interesting night as I'd be given the unique opportunity to meet some of Charlie's other customers who, like me, were regulars in Charlie's chair, some who have been clients for more than five of the six years Charlie had been a barber. And what an assortment of characters, from all over the world, all walks of life and a variety of professions: a Japanese engineer, Polish cardiologist, local Dutch politician, Canadian oilman, Australian opera singer, South African dancer and an Argentinean lawyer working at the Organisation for the Prohibition of Chemical Weapons. By eight-thirty everyone had arrived and taken seats in the salon facing the back of the shop and Charlie's barber station. The only real change that Charlie had to make was to move his barber chair over just slightly so it sat centered in the room, or center stage. Henny set up his portable digital stage piano just off to the left next to the shampoo bay and that was it, nothing fancy because the place was already fancy and already a barbershop with all the furnishings and accoutrements. It was a pretty cool sight to see all of the other customers introducing themselves and mingling as I thought to myself the only thing these guys have in common is Charlie—well, at least in this context anyway—and it was probably highly unlikely that these twelve guys would have ever crossed paths otherwise. I went into the waiting room to give a final look at the refreshment table and I saw Charlie through the French doors that separated the waiting room from the kitchen/bathroom area which was closed off from the salon by a swinging wood door. Charlie was gesturing for me to come, so I walked into the kitchen. *There's one other thing I forgot to mention*, said Charlie. ***You're*** *the customer tonight.* I should have known that Charlie would spring something like that on me so I wasn't at all surprised by his proclamation. I did think how cool that might actually be and I suppose I admit to feeling somewhat honored that Charlie, out of all his more longtime customers, would ask me, the new guy.

The show was nothing less than sensational and from my vantage point in the barber chair, I spent the entire time looking out at the audience. Judging by the expressions on their faces, their reactions and the thunderous applause at the end, Charlie had himself one hell of a successful show. Afterwards, everyone grabbed drinks and plates of cheese, crackers and homemade brownies and peanut butter and chocolate chip oatmeal cookies made by Charlie's daughters. They took their seats once again and Charlie took center stage and sat in his barber chair, only his water bottle in hand as he was too adrenalized to grab anything to eat. For the next forty-five minutes, feedback and opinions were shared though not one single negative comment was uttered, and I felt every comment was sincere and that no one was holding back anything for fear of hurting Charlie's feelings. It was a really good show, an excellent performance and, strange enough, it was just Charlie doing what he always does, cutting hair and telling stories; well, okay, so he doesn't sing while he cuts hair and tells stories, but I think I share everyone's sentiment when I say he sings beautifully and has a wonderful voice. Who would have ever thought?

Charlie organized two more test shows on the last two Saturday evenings of the month, inviting both regular customers and friends to see his performance and give their feedback after the show. I attended the second one and it was just as good as the first one, better maybe, but I can't put my finger on exactly how. Charlie's energy was off the charts and as I looked around, the reactions of smiles, laughs and applause were hearty, frequent and sincere. After the three test shows, Charlie was ready for the next step. He started preparing posters that he uploaded on various social media platforms, especially the dozen or so expat groups he belonged to on Facebook. He started with two Saturday evening performances on alternating weekends and charged twenty-five euros, which included a glass of Cava and these cute little cakes with Adam Driver's likeness printed on the frosting. He also added an additional six chairs that he borrowed from the restaurant next door to up the total capacity to eighteen. His total take for each performance was 450 euros, of which fifty went to pay the rental on the shop, fifty for refreshments, twenty for Henny's taxi (for transporting the digital piano) and 150 for Henny's accompaniment. After setting aside the 21% Charlie would be required to share with the Dutch tax office, he cleared a total of one hundred and forty-two euros and twenty cents, about half of what he'd clear on a normal night of barbering (but twice as fun and in a fraction of the time).

Charlie's next experiment was to keep to his every other Saturday night show, but to try doing *two* shows each night, one at seven-thirty and the other at ten, in true Night Barber fashion. With two shows, he could more than double his share as he'd only have to increase the other expenses marginally. That worked for Charlie. A few months went by and Charlie had sold out every performance and was ready for the next big move—he was going to take his show to a small local theater.

Charlie's theater of choice was Theater Branoul, a 66-seat venue about a fifteen-minute walk from the barbershop. It was the perfect location, easily accessible from everywhere in the city and had the right feeling and charm of the type of theater Charlie liked—small, intimate and cozy. The cost for renting out the theater would be 350 euros a day, and adding in the other costs for crew and refreshments, Charlie would need to sell at least half of the tickets at full price for every show in order to break even and turn a modest profit. He decided to try, albeit ambitiously, renting out the theater for two days—a Saturday and Sunday—with two performances on Saturday night and a matinee *and* an early evening performance on Sunday. If he could sell enough tickets, the weekend could be a big success, both for Charlie's musical and financially.

Opening night at Theater Branoul was a sell-out and the audience, mostly made up of people who knew Charlie personally—friends, customers, former students and colleagues and their plus-ones—loved the show and demonstrated their adoration with a five-minute standing ovation that brought Charlie to tears. But it was Sunday's crowds that really had Charlie tickled pink as there were fewer audience members that he actually knew personally and the reception was every bit as positive as opening night. Charlie's musical worked, and not only did it work, it seemed to have wide-reaching appeal to both the English-speaking expats as well as the Dutch and other non-native English speakers who attended the performances. Charlie had a winner and now it was time to lay the groundwork for bigger and better things.

CHAPTER FOUR

TAKING IT ON THE ROAD

The next step in Charlie's master plan would be to start booking his show into small theaters around the Netherlands. For this, Charlie decided to hire an agency to handle the bookings and promotion.

Charlie first met Karin in 2014, the year he organized the second edition of his now-defunct singer-songwriter festival in The Hague. Karin had heard about the festival and was delighted when she got the news that she was invited to perform at three of the festival's seven venues on two different evenings. On the opening night of the festival, Charlie was making his rounds, popping into all the venues to meet as many of the artists as he could. Walking into the Paard Café just after ten p.m., Charlie stopped as a hauntingly beautiful song was wafting out from behind the wall of the main room. He asked the volunteer at the welcome desk who the performer was on stage and the young woman, looking at her schedule, replied, "that's Karin Kahlert. She just went on." Charlie walked into the room and saw Karin standing on the stage wearing a simple, hunter green, long narrow skirt with a white blouse buttoned up and closed at the neck and a pair of cordovan loafers. She was playing what Charlie immediately recognized as a beautiful mahogany Martin J-15 acoustic guitar and singing a song that Charlie was sure he remembered hearing on one of the hundreds of audition tapes he was sent from prospective singer-songwriters. That song had stuck out to Charlie as having been something very special and now he was watching as the songwriter performed it right before his eyes.

Charlie met Karin right about the time his relationship with the mother of his younger daughters was going through a rough spot, just about nine months before his youngest daughter was born. And while Charlie found himself immediately attracted to her, he was still in a committed relationship and Karin, he thought, must have been at least twenty years younger than he was and that didn't sit too well with him. Over the next decade, Karin continued her singer-songwriter career by playing small clubs and venues all around the world, booking herself into venues from Austria to Australia, playing her brand of original ballads and folk-infused pop while seeing the world. And she did this merely by having the savvy—and *chutzpah*—to reach out to venues directly posing, for lack of a better word, as her own booking agent. She had a professional looking press kit, a designated email address and phone number and knew the ins and outs enough to get herself booked into to top venues. She even opened up for Colombian singer and musician Juanes on the first six nights of his Latin American tour replacing Mexican singer Ximena Sariñana, who took ill on the eve of the tour conveniently the very same day Karin's email landed in the tour manager's inbox. After traveling the world, Karin returned to the Netherlands and set up her own booking agency in The Hague and began promoting singer-songwriters, and herself—and then Charlie, her first theatrical client. Charlie reached out to her as he knew she would be the right person for the job of handling his bookings. She was smart, well connected and knew the ropes (and yes, if you read on, Charlie and Karin ended up together, marrying a few years later, Charlie adopting Karin's seven-year-old son, a boy the same age as Charlie was when his mother's new husband adopted him).

Karin and Charlie's professional relationship hit the ground running as she loved the show and knew she could book it into just about any city or town in the Netherlands, perhaps even Belgium, France and Spain, where there were large communities of English-speaking expats who would certainly enjoy the show. And seeing how the musical was virtually self-contained and easy to move around, build up and break down, Karin saw there was money to be made, even by booking the show into small venues.

Charlie's first performance outside of The Hague was at the Betty Asfalt Complex, a charming 80-seat theater inside an 18th century listed building in Amsterdam's Old West district, a few blocks away from the Anne Frank House and Museum. While the show was big success, it almost didn't happen. Just as Charlie was waiting for Erik, his man-with-a-van, to pick him and his barber chair and portable piano up, he got a call from Henny who had suddenly fallen ill and would be unable to make the show. Staying calm, Charlie called Karin and told her about Henny and she told Charlie to get to Amsterdam and by the time he arrived at the venue, everything would be sorted out. Karin immediately started going through her Amsterdam contacts and found a young Spanish pianist she had met at a recital one of her friends had given a few months earlier. He was available and agreed to meet Charlie at the theater. Karin emailed the song charts to Imanol and after only a single run-through, the show was back on track with a few hours to kill before showtime.

Over the next few months, Charlie and Karin began seeing each other on a regular basis, discussing his performance schedule and plans for the near future, but soon their professional meetings and correspondences became laced with more personal and romantic undertones and before long it was obvious the two were becoming quite fond of each other. One day, Charlie arrived at the barbershop to find a large bouquet of fresh red roses had been delivered. Surprised and intrigued by who could have sent the flowers, he rushed to open the small envelope that was inserted into the bouquet. On the tiny white card was nothing more than a single initial, written in cursive with a medium-tipped black marker...*K*. And from that day forward, he would call Karin 'K', and over time, she would become the love of his life, his best friend, companion and business partner.

Charlie continued working as The Night Barber, but thanks to the success of his musical there was now greater demand for his services as a barber. K. convinced Charlie to leave the comfort of the hair salon and open his own barbershop and bring on a few barbers and extend the opening hours from noon until midnight, seven days a week, meaning that not only was Charlie the only barber in town offering after-hours service, he was now offering it every day—and night—of the week. He opened a small, but elegant two-chair barbershop in the fashionable Royal Shopping District in The Hague, near to Sam's old shop where he had trained years earlier. He hired three barbers to split the shifts and an apprentice to learn the trade and serve as an assistant to the barbers, doing shampoos, blow drying, finishing and providing hospitality to the clients. As soon as the barbershop in The Hague was up and running, Charlie and K. found a charming little storefront in Amsterdam, hired a team of four barbers—one who would act as the shop manager—and hung his Night Barber shingle there.

It wasn't before long that, thanks to K.'s business acumen, they started selling franchise-style partnerships to barbers in New York City, Chicago, Los Angeles, London and Berlin and The Night Barber was quickly becoming a recognized and trusted global name in the industry. They also started selling their own branded products—hair pomade, beard oil, shampoo, shaving cream and a whole range of men's grooming supplies—all with the distinctive Night Barber logo and all being sustainably manufactured using the highest quality organic and vegan ingredients.

Now that a steady revenue stream was established, K. suggested that Charlie focus on getting back to his original plan, to getting his screenplay of *A Return to Paterson* made into a film. The idea was to start work on getting the one-man musical to New York and by hook or by crook using it as a vehicle to get the attention of Adam Driver (or anyone else in the business who would be willing to champion the project). Surely, somehow Driver would discover a play that had his very name in the title, be intrigued and go check it out. And that was exactly how Charlie had envisioned the whole thing coming to fruition. Charlie called Abbott and told him he was ready for phase two, ready to take his one-man musical to New York and asked Abbott if he'd join him on an exploratory trip to scout out small, off-off-Broadway theaters and start setting things in motion. Abbott was keen to sign on and was enthusiastic about the prospect of going to New York with Charlie, and seeing how his daughter lived there, he'd save

Charlie the added expense of room and board. Abbott was also keen to re-kindle some old friendships and to visit some of the old haunts from his days as a directing student at Boston University in the 1970s, and later when he returned in the early 80s painting scenery in non-union shops, assisting off-Broadway designers and washing buckets at the Metropolitan Opera.

Charlie and Abbott met at Dublin Airport to catch their flight to New York. Upon arrival, Abbott went directly to his daughter's apartment to drop off his things while Charlie checked in at the CitizenM Hotel in Times Square, his home for the next seven days. The hotel was a short eight-minute walk to the 65-seat Sargent Theater, located in The American Theater of Actors complex on West 54th Street in the old 7th District police court building adjacent to the current NYPD 18th Precinct station. While Charlie and Abbott had meetings at no less than six other theaters that week, Charlie secretly had his heart set on the Sargent for his play, as he was very fond of the small theater since first seeing *Found a Peanut*, by Donald Margulies, there in June of 1989. That was when Charlie finished his first year as a playwriting major and spent a week in New York City, where he saw four plays, two musicals and attended an evening of staged readings by up and coming playwrights at the Dramatists Guild headquarters at 1501 Broadway. After he checked in at the hotel, he walked over to the Dunkin' Donuts at 51st and 8th and ordered an oat milk latte and two Boston cream donuts and called K. as he sat looking out at the Gershwin Theater, dreaming that one day the name of his musical would be on that marquee.

Charlie and Abbott had a productive week and—to no one's surprise—ended up signing a rental agreement to hire out the Sargent Theater for three nights at the end of October. They spent their evenings like kids in a candy store, seeing plays, eating out and meeting up with old friends. Charlie even had lunch one afternoon at Liebman's Deli in the Bronx with Dan Levine, who played trombone in Charlie's 80s new wave band, Café Society. During the week, Charlie also called in on his business partner Avram, who was now running two Night Barber shops in Midtown East and the Upper West Side. Charlie was thrilled to see his concept working so well in New York and was filled with pride after visiting the shops and having the chance to meet some of the barbers and even talk with a few customers. Avram pulled Charlie aside and asked how things went with the theaters. When Charlie told him they had hired the Sargent, Avram said, "put me down for twenty-five tickets on opening night, I'm going to close the shops early and take my guys on a night out to see a play written and starring the founder of The Night Barber." Charlie was overrun with emotion and thanked Avram, giving him a hug and thanking him for all he had done and for his support of the play. At least, Charlie thought to himself, they'll be twenty-five people in the audience on opening night.

The week flew by and Charlie headed back home to the Netherlands, while Abbott stayed on for another ten days. Charlie returned to work at the barbershop and in between work and a steady performance schedule of three shows on alternating weekends in Dutch cities all across the country, he also got busy writing a new song for the musical. Charlie intended on adding an additional ten minutes to the total performance time, making a slightly longer show as he thought it would be more appealing and serve to justify the twenty-five-euro ticket price. Once the song was finished, he made a quick recording of it and emailed it to Henny, who called the next day saying he had finished it and would come over to try it out with Charlie that afternoon. The show was now about eighty minutes in duration and would take Charlie a month of rehearsals and classes with his vocal coach Maurits to build up the chops he needed to do a longer show. Charlie realized, as he pushed towards sixty-five, that his physical limitations were waning, that the aches and pains of aging were slowly creeping up on him. But that didn't diminish his drive and he was grateful for being able to experience a creative renaissance when most men his age were slipping quietly into retirement, playing golf or going on cruises. But certainly, the one thing Charlie didn't expect to happen at his age, was to become a father again, and when K. told him she was expecting a baby the next spring, he was ecstatic, but cautiously wondering to himself whether he thought he'd be able to raise another child with the vim and vigor he had five times before. They talked about it at length and concluded it was god's will and the couple would now reveal the news to their respective families. The third act of Charlie's life was starting to take shape in ways he never could have imagined, and he was happier than he'd ever been.

The summer came and went and Charlie was preparing for his New York debut. The first part of his plan was set and now he had to start thinking of ways to make certain Adam Driver would catch wind of the show and be curious enough to buy a ticket and come to the theater, where Charlie would choose the actor as his audience participating customer, sit him in the chair and, finally, pitch his idea for the *Paterson* sequel. He knew Driver lived in Brooklyn Heights, so he had to make sure that posters of the play would be strategically placed around the neighborhood, increasing the odds that Driver would see them. K. got in touch with her friend Mallory, who was a publicist in New York, who booked ads in *Time Out* and the *Brooklyn Heights Press*, amongst other local publications. Driver was sure to get wind of the play and even if he didn't see the ads or posters, certainly someone he knew would and then convey it to Driver. And that's exactly what happened. That summer, Driver was traveling to Europe to promote the newly released *Heat 2*, the prequel to Michael Mann's 1995 crime film starring Al Pacino, Robert De Niro and an all-star cast, where Driver plays the young Neil McCauley, the role De Niro originated. So, it happened that Driver's friend, and another famous resident of Brooklyn Heights, actor Ethan Hawke, saw a poster for the play at the corner deli on State and Henry and snapped a photo of it on his phone and sent it to Driver in Italy. I won't go into how I came upon that little tidbit, but I thought I'd throw it into the story as it will make sense a little later.

Rehearsals were in full swing by the end of the summer and Abbott had flown over from Zurich to see how things were getting on. Henny, who had never been to the U.S., was busy getting his visas in order and was excited about the trip, seeing New York and playing in a New York theater, even if it was only an off-off-Broadway theater. As an added bonus, Charlie told Henny that he would be paying for Henny to bring his wife and daughter along on the trip, joking that he would cover all his expenses but that Henny would be picking up the tab for pierogis, borscht and *medovyk*, the traditional Ukrainian layered honey and sour cream cake, at Veselka, the oldest

Ukrainian restaurant in New York City over on 2nd Avenue.

The New York debut of *Adam Driver and the Million Dollar Haircut* was to take place on Halloween night, with one show at eight p.m. followed by a Saturday evening performance and two shows on Sunday, a matinee at two-thirty and the closing performance of the run at eight. As time drew nearer, Charlie found a moment of respite while out on his daily walk along the waterway near his house, where he would often go to clear his mind amongst the trees and water while tallying his 20,000 steps. As he arrived in the neighboring village of Voorburg, he sat on a bench in front of the old Protestant church and lost himself in a daydream. How amazing, he thought, how incredible this journey has been up until now. Not too many years ago, he was teaching English and selling his bow ties at artisan markets, making school runs and lunches and organizing play dates for his daughters. Then he met Sam, who convinced him to become a barber, who trained him, who encouraged him to take that leap of faith and go into business for himself with his one-of-a-kind Night Barber concept. And now, Charlie was weeks away from bringing his one-man musical, born from the ashes of songs and ideas he had for a very different musical some forty years earlier. He had met Henny, whose musical mastery and no-nonsense way of getting Charlie to toe the line and stay focused had been an indispensable part of Charlie's success. He brought his former college professor-turned friend Abbott on board to direct his play, but got so much more than a director, as Abbott's mentorship and camaraderie proved to be a bedrock of support. And finally, he reconnected and fell in love with K., and that, perhaps more than any other event, fired Charlie up with a level of inspiration that even Charlie himself could have never imagined.

K. had been working to finalize all the last-minute arrangements: hotel bookings, promotions, interviews with the local press, a few theater-focused podcasts, a spa day reservation for herself and Charlie at Aire Ancient Baths in TriBeCa and placing a food order with Whole Foods Market to stock up on drinks and healthy snacks for the green room at the theater. And K. made one final call to Page Sargisson, a jewelry designer in Brooklyn that her friend Mallory, the publicist, recommended who was crafting a custom-made platinum wedding band for Charlie that K. was going to give him when she proposed on that Halloween morning during breakfast at Friedman's in Hell's Kitchen. She'd been planning to propose to Charlie for months and couldn't think of a better time or place to do it than at breakfast, Charlie's favorite meal and the one time he set aside every day to be with K. and their children. And she felt the backdrop of New York and the excitement of Charlie's play opening the perfect time to make it known to Charlie—and the world—that she planned on spending the rest of her life with him, as his wife, partner, friend and companion.

By mid-October, Charlie had finished the last performances of the year in the Netherlands and had hired a barber to pick up most of his appointments straight through until the week before Christmas, when Charlie would work twelve-hour days for two weeks straight making sure all of his long-time regulars—the ones who would only let Charlie cut their hair—got their fresh holiday haircuts and beard trims. On the Monday before the big New York premiere (for Charlie, it might as well have been at the Majestic instead of the off-off-Broadway Sargent Theater) Charlie and K. took the kids—Charlie's three daughters and K.'s son—out to dinner at Señor Torres, their favorite Venezuelan restaurant owned by Antonio Torres, a longtime customer and friend of Charlie's, for a pre-New York trip celebration. Charlie, lost in thought as he so often was, sat there and watched as the four people he loved more than anything enjoying *tequeños, mandocas, tajadas, arepas, yucas fritas* and the best *tarta tres leches* this side of Caracas, while Charlie was overcome with a sense that nothing could be better than this moment, not even a standing ovation on opening night in New York City. This was Charlie's time, the moment he'd been waiting for all his life. All the gigs with his band back in L.A. in the 1980s; all the writing he'd submitted over the years, the rejection letters and unfulfilled dreams of becoming a great writer or musician; his failed relationships and other losses. None of that seemed to matter to Charlie now as he took his spoonful of milky sponge cake and final sip of espresso. K. did everything in her power to keep Charlie calm and focused that week as she sensed he was more nervous than usual which, she figured, was normal and to be expected under the circumstances. On Tuesday morning, Charlie had a session with his voice coach then went into the shop for a haircut, bringing sandwiches and salads for lunch for the guys on the afternoon shift. Then, on the way home, he stopped off at P.W. Akkerman where he bought a Montblanc Meisterstück Solitaire Legrand pen as a gift he would give to Henny on opening night.

Charlie and K. met Henny and his wife and daughter at the train station on Wednesday morning and headed for Schiphol Airport in Amsterdam for their one p.m. flight to

New York. They arrived at JFK around three p.m. and were met by Abbott, who had arrived from Zurich a few hours earlier and who had rented an eight-passenger Chevrolet Express that would get them into and around town for the next eight days. After checking in at their respective hotels, they met for dinner at Guy Vaknin's vegan, kosher Italian eatery Coletta on 3rd Avenue in Gramercy. Guy was a friend of Charlie's New York partner, Avram, who made the reservation telling Vaknin how Charlie was going to be the next Stephen Sondheim, so he'd better give him and his party the best table in the joint (as well as two bottles of Tenuta Santome Prosecco, courtesy of Avram himself).

On Thursday morning, everyone had breakfast at their respective lodgings and met at the theater at eleven, where they were greeted by Pauline, the theater manager, and Sonia who, with Gustavo, her intern, ran the lighting and sound. Over coffee and biscotti from Scotto's they went over all the particulars and updates on ticket sales—Friday night's premiere and Saturday night's performance were sold out and there were still some tickets unsold for Sunday's matinee and evening show, but Pauline was confident that they would sell out as well. At eleven-thirty, the van arrived from Avram's barbershop museum where he had kept nearly every barber chair, station, mirror, barber pole, clipper, trimmer, scissors and hundreds of accoutrements from the barbershop his father first opened when Avram's family immigrated to the United States from Uzbekistan in the 1980s. A fourth generation master barber, Avram had also been collecting barbershop memorabilia for the past dozen years, showing them off on his frequent appearances on local morning news programs, radio interviews and podcasts talking about the rich history of barbers and barbershops in New York. The first thing that Avram's guys unloaded from the van was the centerpiece of the show, a 1908 Koken barber chair in tufted black leather upholstery with ivory-colored painted metal, glistening chrome and one hundred silver rivets on the seat, seat back, foot rest and leg support. Next, they loaded in a beautiful antique hutch with a rose-tinted mirror that was from Avram's father's original barbershop at 290 Columbus Avenue. After the chair and hutch were set up at center stage, Avram wheeled in a large steamer trunk on a dolly that contained all the barber tools Charlie would need for the show. Finally, the barber pole was brought in and when Charlie saw it for the first time he was overwhelmed with emotion at the sight of the six-foot tall, hand-painted, red and white pole with its royal blue turned ball finial top and matching wrought iron legs. Avram had come through in grand style, just as he said he would and no less than Charlie would have expected from his friend who lived and breathed the barber's life. And to his express his gratitude, albeit in a very modest way, Charlie donated a portion of the proceeds from Sunday's matinee to the community daycare center Avram supported.

With the load-in complete, it was time for lunch and Charlie had pizzas, salads, eggplant Parmigiana and a tray of homemade tiramisu brought in from Ray's in Times Square. After lunch, Charlie and Henny were scheduled to do a run-through while the crew tested the lights and sound. With six hours to go before their opening night eve preview—to be attended by family, friends, members of the press and a small contingency of drama students from the New York Conservatory for Dramatic Arts—Charlie was starting to feel the rush of adrenaline beginning to flow through his veins and he was pumped and ready to go. Charlie looked on as his partners in crime sat around the stage eating and drinking and talking amongst themselves. He felt that even if some catastrophic event occurred at that very moment and the shows were canceled, he'd still be happy, thrilled the way everything had turned out and pleased beyond words how, by merely watching a film just a few years earlier, his life had come full circle and he had achieved more than he could have possibly ever imagined.

I suppose you could say this is my favorite part of the story. Not only because what I'm about to tell you is the story of how, after everything that Charlie had lived and experienced in his life came together on one magical and unforgettable night in New York City, but how *I* came to literally be part of that story.

I had just got home from work and my wife told me I had a call from my barber in New York City. Surprised, I immediately checked my phone but there were no messages—text, voice or otherwise—and no emails in my inbox. How odd, I thought, that Charlie would call me on my house phone, but he did leave a number with instructions to call him as soon as I got his message. I called Charlie who said he was in a van being driven somewhere in Brooklyn Heights. Then he dropped the bomb.

"Casper," he said in a tone of voice that was both authoritative and soft. "Do you remember when I first told you about my crazy idea about writing the musical?" he asked.

"Sure," I replied.

"And do you remember what I told when you said you would be the first person to buy a ticket for opening night when it went to Broadway?"

"Of course, I do," I said. "You told me that the day your play opened on Broadway, you would not only buy me a front row ticket, but pay for my flight, hotel and meals."

"Good memory," said Charlie. "Well, I know you said Broadway, but would you consider off-off-Broadway as still being Broadway?"

It turned out that Charlie had overlooked something. Back home in The Hague, whenever Charlie had a show, he'd reach out to one of his regulars to sit in the chair for the duration of the show and get a free cut while Charlie told his stories and sung his songs. And when he traveled, he usually used local contacts to secure an able and willing "customer" who wouldn't mind a few dozen theatergoers looking his way while he had his hair cut. But he really didn't know many people in New York, not well enough anyway to reach out to and this wasn't just any show, this was his New York, off-off-Broadway debut and, as his nine out of ten on the scale of nervousness was edging north, he began to panic. *If only Casper could be here*, he thought to himself. *It would be like the old days, like the very day I first told him—told anyone—my idea about the musical.*

"What would it take for me to get you over here?" Charlie enquired, this being the last thing I ever expected he would ask. I was at a loss for words. I asked Charlie if he could give me ten minutes to talk to my wife and look over my agenda and get right back to him. He told me he'd call me back in thirty minutes and not to worry if I couldn't make it happen. As it turned out, there was nothing too urgent that couldn't be moved to the following week and my wife was on board knowing how cool of an experience this would be. Charlie called a half an hour later, just as he said he would, and I told him I'd get the next flight to New York. I also told him I had one condition for my coming over and that was I pay my own way. He grappled with my demand for a moment and agreed, though I knew it wouldn't be last I'd be hearing of it. I was going to New York. To see my barber for a haircut. And take part in the single most important moment of his career as a playwright, composer, actor and singer. And I was going to be the guy in the chair on opening night.

I arrived in New York some fifteen hours later and Charlie was there at the airport with Abbott, who I'd met at the first test shows at the barbershop back in The Hague. The CitizenM where Charlie and K. were staying was full, so I booked myself in at the Hard Rock Hotel just around the corner on 48th Street. They dropped me off at the hotel and told me to be at the theater around seven, that there would be food and drink and that we'd go out to eat a proper meal after the performance and roundtable discussion with the audience that followed.

Arriving at the theater complex I found my way to Charlie, who was in the dressing room doing some vocal warmups in between gargles of warm salt water. We talked for a few minutes and he told me how glad he was that I flew over and hoped it would all be worth my time, effort and expense. I asked him if he knew anything about Adam Driver, was he able to make contact or find a way to invite him to the show. He said he'd exhausted about every hairbrained idea he could think of—including putting up posters in his neighborhood—but would have to wait out the weekend and be patient, hoping that somehow the actor found out about the show and decided to come and check it out.

The preview was great and Charlie was in top form. What a difference, I thought to myself, from those early days of merely talking about doing it and those crude first shows at the barbershop which, while good enough—and they were—it was so amazing to see how much the show had evolved from that point to where it was now, and I couldn't have felt more privileged to be a part of it—to have *been* a part it—from the very beginning. After the theater had cleared out and Charlie changed out of his barber costume (which I guess, Charlie being a *real* barber after all, can't really be considered a costume!), he, Henny (his wife and daughter went back to the hotel after the show), K., Abbott, Sophia, Gustavo and I walked over to RT60, on the 34th floor of the Hard Rock Hotel, where I was staying, and gorged ourselves on small bites of tuna tacos, oysters, Wagyu sliders, poke bowls, mezze plates, *tres leches* cake and Key lime tart. And after our smorgasbord-style meal, we sat around until nearly two a.m. sipping Patrón Reposado finishing, between the six of us, every drop of the four-hundred-and twenty-five-dollar bottle of tequila.

Charlie, despite going to sleep just before three a.m., was up bright eyed and bushy tailed at eight and was downstairs at the breakfast buffet while K. was still tossing and turning in bed. He hit the buffet hard, piling on a mountain of scrambled eggs that would keep his energy up until lunchtime; an everything bagel, *pain au chocolat* and a cappuccino rounded out his breakfast and had him feeling ready for the day. Friday morning's eleven o'clock call at the theater was more a business affair rather than a creative one, except for the photo shoot and visit from the piano tuner and a technician who was doing something or another with an electrical panel backstage. Charlie was already in full Charlie mode, joking nervously, cracking one-liners and clinging ever so close to K. who, aware of his agitations and anxiety, knew how to keep Charlie calm and focused. Charlie called me around noon to make sure I was up and not too hungover, seeing how I had one too many tequila shots the night before. Surprisingly, I was fine, thanks to an expensive bottle of tequila and the fact that I'd had quite a good amount of food for the booze to mingle nicely with. Charlie said everyone was meeting at Friedman's for lunch around one and I told him I'd see him there. Meanwhile, I showered, read the paper and had a leisurely walk through Times Square, arriving at the restaurant just as Charlie and company were walking in the door, the only newcomer to the crowd being Abbott's daughter, whom I had never met before. At lunch, I couldn't take my eyes off of Charlie, who was now more relaxed and seemed to really be living in the moment. And in a half sort of daydream, I wondered what Charlie was like as a kid, a teenager and young adult. I've heard him tell so many stories about his life that sometimes it was hard to believe one person could have lived so many lives, had so many incredible experiences and still be looking for and wanting more. Charlie thought of himself as an everyman, as a regular guy who was just restless enough, curious enough and crazy enough to try everything at least once, and it worked for Charlie and Charlie ended up creating for himself a most extraordinary life, one that didn't earn him fame or fortune, but one whose rewards were, in a way, bigger and better than all the fame and fortune in the world. In the end, he followed his heart and dreams, he loved and was loved and raised a bunch of kids who, from the looks of things, inherited their father's zest for life. So, what more could he have possibly wanted? I think what Charlie wanted most was to re-connect with his son and maybe he thought by achieving the kind of success he was on the cusp of achieving, it might bring his son around, might make him proud of his father just enough to give him a second chance.

After lunch, Charlie went back to the hotel and took a nap, waking up around four then going downstairs for an iced latte and a chocolate brownie. K. joined him and the two spent the next half hour going over some of K.'s notes and selecting some of the stories Charlie would add to his rotating repertoire. I found this aspect of Charlie's show to be the most remarkable. The show had no script, per se, but on the other hand it wasn't improvised either. Early on in the show's development, Abbott had suggested that Charlie throw out the script he had written and simply perform the show as Charlie the Barber, his character in the show because, after all, the two were one and the same. So, before every show, Charlie would sit down and pick the stories he was going to use in that evening's performance; sure, there was a base of stories that made up the foundation of the show and those were in every performance, but he switched around the anecdotes and mixed things up, making every show spontaneous and a unique experience even for spectators who had already seen the show before. And not unlike his barbershop customers, Charlie saw many of the same people coming back two or three times to see his show, knowing that each time they'd discover something new.

Friday night's call was at six and Charlie was already in his dressing room when I arrived at the theater at a quarter to. Abbott and Henny were in the dressing room and the three men were gathered over and glancing onto the screen of Charlie's iPad. Charlie waved me over and what they were looking at was director Michael Mann's Instagram account where they were scrolling through photos of Adam Driver from Mann's 2023 film *Ferrari*, starring Driver as race car driver Enzo Ferrari, founder of the motor racing team and automobile brand that bears his name. Then, scrolling towards the top of the page were photos—photos dated as recently as the past few days—of Mann and Driver promoting their film *Heat 2* in Rome, Madrid and Lisbon. Did that mean Driver was still abroad? That he wasn't in New York and that there would be no chance (even though it was already a near impossibility) that Driver would attend one of this weekend's performances? Despite what Charlie had seen online, he was in an upbeat *the show must go on* frame of mind, excited in almost a boyish way, grinning and nodding at me every now again just as he'd been grinning and nodding at everyone that day. I knew as much as he wanted Adam Driver to show up in the audience and call him up on stage and sit him down in his barber chair and tell him his idea about the sequel to *Paterson*, I was convinced that whether or not Driver actually came, Charlie was going to give one hundred and ten percent to his performance as he always did.

By seven-thirty, the theater was nearly at capacity and a few folding chairs were brought in and set up at the front of the room and quickly occupied by, of all people, Birgitta Tazelaar, the Dutch Ambassador to the United States, her husband and two of their four children, who Charlie had invited but, probably for security reasons, did not respond to the invitation. K. put a bit of makeup on me and Henny before sitting down and doing Charlie's makeup and hair.

And like always, there was 80s new wave music on in the background playing The Lightning Seeds, Tears For Fears, U2 and Duran Duran. Abbott came into the dressing at a quarter to eight with the fifteen-minute call and Charlie stood up and began his pre-show ritual of a minute of silent reflection while doing some stretches followed by a long hug with K. Charlie walked backstage and at a minute past eight saw the lights dim and heard the murmur of the audience subside until there was total silence and darkness in the house. Then, the light from the wall-mounted barber pole lit up and Henny walked out from behind the curtain and sat down at the Yamaha baby grand piano at stage right and began to play the opening sonata, the piano interlude of *Phone Call, Phone Call.* After the 32-bar cut, Charlie walks on stage, looks into the mirror as he buttons up his pristine white barber's jacket, sprays some tonic on his hair and combs it down then splashing a palmful of shaving lotion on his face before noticing the audience and breaking the fourth wall by addressing the crowd directly…

Oh, hello! I didn't notice you there, I don't actually open up for business for another fifteen minutes. But that's okay, sit, stay where you are, I'm just getting ready for my first customer. I'm Charlie, by the way, Charlie the Barber and this is my shop. I'm known as The Night Barber because, well, I guess it's pretty obvious because I work evenings. Of course, my name's not really Charlie, but it will be for the next hour or so. I chose the name Charlie the Barber for my character because, well, I play a barber—I mean, I am a barber in real life but I'm playing the role of a barber in this…anyway, where was I? Right. Charlie the Barber. So, I named my character Charlie the Barber after a character my favorite actor plays in a film. In this particular film the character's name is Charlie Barber. Charlie's not a barber in the film, he's a director, a theatre director, you know, like New York theater, Broadway! In the film, Charlie's going through a pretty messy divorce with his wife Nicole, who's an actor, I mean, she's an actor in the film and in this film, she's just acted in Charlie's latest play that wins Charlie a big grant so he can take the play to Broadway. I hope that's not too confusing. Anybody know the film I'm talking about? Exactly, 'Marriage Story,' written and directed by Noah Baumbach and released in 2019 starring Adam Driver and Scarlett Johansson. Alan Alda and Ray Liotta were also in the film and Laura Dern, who played Scarlett Johansson's character Nicole's lawyer in the film won the Oscar for best supporting actress that year. And speaking of films, I've been watching films—and loving films—my whole life, like I imagine most of us have; films that, during every stage of my life have had an impact and played an important part in my life. And there have been some films that, as one might imagine, have made a more profound impact than others. For example, 'Bullitt', directed by Peter Yates and starring Steve McQueen, released in 1968, when I was merely a boy of five years old (and how, why and who would take a five-year-old to see a murder-filled action thriller?). Well, my grandfather, actually. He was the quintessential traveler. And when, in the winter of 1968, he wanted to go to Miami Beach for a week and his wife—my grandmother—had work and a busy social calendar, five-year-old me was as good a travel companion as any (at least my grandfather thought so!). So, we packed up and flew down to Miami, staying, as one did back in the day, at the famous Fontainebleau Hotel (with its equally famous talking parrot in the lobby) and kicked back for a week of swimming pools, breakfasts at Sambos and a trip to Key West, which was dampened, so to speak, by a rare tropical winter storm that had us evacuated in a kind Samaritan's van. One hot day, my grandfather decided he had had enough of the heat and storms and decided to go to the movies and cool off. Thinking it would also be a nice refreshing atmosphere for his young travel companion to have a nap, he chose the closest movie theatre to the hotel which happened to be showing 'Bullitt', and we ended up sitting through three full showings of the one-hundred-thirteen-minute film! Needless to say, even at five, the film made a big impression, especially the famous car chase scene through the streets of San Francisco and the scene where McQueen shoots actor Pat Renella who goes crashing through the glass doors at San Francisco International Airport. Right. Anyway. What was I talking about? Oh, right. 'Marriage Story', Adam Driver…So, I saw this film and up until that moment I'd never seen Driver in a film, though I actually had, but didn't remember as his small role in Steven Spielberg's 'Lincoln,' where he played the telegraph operator Samuel something or another, didn't really catch my attention at the time. And of course, Driver came to worldwide renown for his portrayal of Kylo Ren in those 'Star Wars' films, which I also didn't see. I was totally taken by Driver's stellar performance in 'Marriage Story' and loved the film though I barely managed to watch it with a dry eye as the theme brought back sad recollections of my own failed first marriage and divorce. And adding to the despair was Driver's uncanny resemblance to my own son, with whom I had been estranged since the start of the COVID-19 pandemic. But I guess that's another story for another time…So, I imagine many of you might be wondering what's the million-dollar haircut and what does it have to do with Adam Driver? And I hope to answer that question in the next hour and a bit though it's complicated and I tend to be long-winded in my explanations and frequently go off topic—as if you hadn't already noticed. I like to think of myself as being a good storyteller, I mean, that's why my customers keep coming back. Oh, I'm a decent enough barber (though I haven't been one for long as I spent twenty-six years working as teacher), but I'm pretty sure most of my customers come back because one, I'm the only barber who cuts hair in town four nights a week until midnight; two, because I play great music (nothing but 80s new wave though I have been known to play Chet Baker from time to time); three, can converse on an endless number of topics and, four, believe it or not, I'm actually a very good listener (despite being a windbag) and have heard it all, from marriages, divorce, births, deaths, depression and suicidal ideation, to getting new jobs, getting fired from old jobs and everything in between. But I think it's my gift of gab and being able to tell a good story, one that resonates with people, that keep bringing my customers back.

Henny begins to play while Charlie grabs the broom and sweeps the shop floor before breaking into the show's first musical number, *The Storyteller*…

> *I've got a funny way of telling a story*
> *I speak too quickly and my thoughts go astray*
> *Forget where I've come from, forget where I'm going*
> *I make up my stories along the way*
>
> *I've got this crazy way of telling a story*
> *It's like a mishmash that actually makes sense*
> *It starts in the middle and ends like a riddle*

I hurry and scurry and do so without pretense

No offense (I mean)
We're all friends (how keen!)
Stay with me 'til the end(ing)

I'm gonna to find a way of telling my story
So, when it's over you'll be glad that you came
Glad that you came and glad that you stayed
With no regret for all the money you paid

All the money
Milk and honey
All the cash I made!

Here's the serious part of the song
Played in a minor key that really doesn't belong
But then again who's to say what's right and what is wrong
It's nice because it's the part where everyone sways and sings along

La la la la la
La la la la la...

Gotta find a way to continue my story
The clock is ticking and there's so much to say
So many stories, I don't want to be boring
No sleeping! No snoring!! Hey you, put that phone away!!!

Put your phones down
Wipe away your sad frowns

Sit up straight, feet flat on the ground!

Now it's time to get on with the story
Thank you all for coming I truly hope you'll enjoy
At the end of the session, I'll expect an ovation
A pause for guffaws with a flourish of thunderous
applause

Henny continues with a melodic fade out while Charlie picks up the monologue where it left off…

I've always dreamed about that, ever since I was little kid, singing the opening number in a big Broadway musical and standing in the footlights while the audience roared and applause reverberated throughout the theater. But that dream, like so many dreams, is long gone. I'm in my 60s now. 60s. I still can't believe it. 60 years of…well, living, doing what living people do. Going to school, getting a job, marriage, children, retirement. And that's what I decided to do in 2018. Well, not really retire in the literal sense. But retire from a career I'd had for more than 25 years…I was a teacher, like I said. Started off as a late bloomer going to graduate school in my early thirties, doing my teacher training at, of all places, the very same Chicago Public High School where, eleven years earlier, I graduated in the bottom half of the bottom half of my graduating class at the school where I was nothing more than an underachiever; few friends, fewer ambitions and not a whole lot of promise to excel at anything…I moved to L.A. after high school, started my own new wave band, Café Society, my girlfriend from back home moved out there a year later once she graduated from high school and things were actually starting to look up. I had a good job—a few good jobs—in banking and retail, and my band was starting to take off. We even opened up for the Red Chili Peppers a million times, though they weren't as famous back then as they were to become. You know, their lead singer Anthony Kiedis once introduced us as the greatest opening band in L.A. I guess that was meant as a compliment, though thinking about in retrospect, opening bands never really got anywhere, rarely became headliners like the Chili Peppers and more often than not never got signed to record deals or made it to the bigtime. But I loved being the frontman of a band; playing guitar and singing songs I wrote was amazing. But I guess, looking back now, I wasn't as aggressive as I needed to be to take things to the next level. I suppose you could say I focused more on my nine-to-five job and making sure the bills were paid and food was on the table. But I wouldn't have traded those five or six years for anything and to this day I still refer to those as being the best years of my life. And that's exactly what the title was of the last song Café Society ever recorded in 1987, one of the original songs I wrote for my musical. While the song wasn't about the band, per se, it was about my breakup from my longtime girlfriend, who I'd known since I was about twelve years old and who was the band's keyboard player until we split up the year before the band came to an end and I moved back to Chicago…So, about the whole Adam Driver connection, why would someone name a musical—and a one-man musical of all odd things—after an actor? And million-dollar haircut? What's that all about? Well, I'll continue where I left off…I always tell people that I came late to the Adam Driver party. He was already what you might consider to be a big movie star by the time I saw him in 'Marriage Story' on Netflix in the summer of 2021. So, the last big lockdown of the pandemic had just ended, I'd gone back to work at the barbershop and it had been more than a year since my son stopped talking to me. And you know something, after all these years, I still can't give you a good reason why, but I gather it was to do with my not reaching out to him at the start of the pandemic. But if I dig deeper I'm sure the problem started years before when his mother and I divorced and I moved away. Though we talked every day and saw each other frequently, I guess the traumas of my leaving and living so far away took their toll and resulted in him simply pulling away from me. Then, one day in September, a new customer showed up at the barbershop and I was pleasantly surprised to find my new client somewhat resembled Adam Driver (who, in turn, somewhat resembled my son). I mean he was a real doppelganger of both of them—tall and lanky, long, wavy hair just above the shoulders and soft-spoken and mild-mannered, just as the actor was on screen and how I imagined he might be in real life, and not too dissimilar from my son's demeanor. Michael was an authentically nice guy and he still comes to the shop with his two young sons, and always brings me a piece of cake or a blondie from the bakery where his wife works. After Michael's first visit, I delved even deeper into the movie world of Adam Driver and started watching all of his films—'Frances Ha', 'This is Where I Leave You', 'The Report', 'The Dead Don't Die', 'BlacKkKlansman'—but the one that stood out from the pack, the film that would forever change my life, was 2016's 'Paterson', written and directed by Jim Jarmusch. Let me just tell you right now that 'Paterson' is probably the most nondescript, uneventful and lackluster film you'll ever see, because it is just that. But at the same time, it's become my favorite film of all time. Here's the story, and believe me when I tell you there's no spoiler alert needed... The film, set in Paterson, New Jersey, in the present, follows seven days in the lives of a young married couple, Paterson—that's Driver's character's name—and his wife Laura, played beautifully by the beautiful French-Iranian actress Golshifteh Farahani. The couple live in a small ranch-style house in suburban Paterson with their English bulldog Marvin, played, incidentally, by a female dog named Nelly in the film who died shortly after the movie was made and was the first canine performer to win a posthumous Palm Dog Award at the Cannes Film Festival. Driver's character is a city bus driver, who drives the number 23 route— curiously enough that's the same route that passes through my suburban neighborhood in the town where I live just outside of The Hague. And even more of a coincidence, I dreamed of being a bus driver when I was a little boy and would often play bus on my grandmother's sideboard, using a round corduroy pillow from the couch and punching real CTA transfers my grandparents would bring home from their daily commutes downtown. And more curious still was the bus that passed through their neighborhood was the number 84 Peterson Avenue bus. Peterson, Paterson, close enough for jazz, right? Or at least for one cool coincidence. When Paterson's not driving his bus, he passes the time writing poems in the style of his favorite poet, William Carlos Williams, who features prominently in the film and not so accurately as having lived and practiced medicine in Paterson, though he was born, lived, practiced medicine and died in nearby Rutherford, New Jersey, about ten miles down the road. His wife Laura is a homemaker, spending her days lost in endless DIY projects, painting, making curtains and painting abstract portraits of Marvin their dog. She also bakes cupcakes for the local Saturday farmer's market and dreams of building a cupcake empire, "getting rich from cupcakes", as she once told her husband. She also dreams of becoming a country singer, "maybe even a big star like one of the greats, like Tammy Wynette or Patsy Cline." And that's the whole film. Paterson wakes up every morning, drives his bus, has lunch packed up in a classic Stanley lunchbox that Laura fills with sandwiches, her homemade cupcakes and a love letter to her beloved husband; he sits in front of the Great Falls of the Passaic River and writes poetry in his 'secret notebook', goes home, has dinner, walks Marvin and stops at Shades Bar for a beer and a chat with owner/barman Doc, before going home and heading off to bed, only to repeat the same events the next day. And the next. For seven days, and the film ends. Well, more or less. So, the more I watched the film—hundreds of times by then—I became more and more taken with the non-story and started to wonder what happened next, what happened on the following day, days, weeks, months and years after the credits rolled. Now that in and of itself is unusual for me as I've never questioned a film that way before; film ends and it ends, you throw the empty popcorn tub away and you go home. But there was something about this film, something I'd never experienced before in all of my years seeing movies. I wanted to know more. I needed to know more. And to satisfy that need, I began concocting all kinds of ideas for an imaginary sequel to the film, coming up with scenes and scenarios and all kinds of storylines to try and satisfy my fascination. Then one day, Michael came into the shop for a haircut and as he sat in my chair, I found myself looking at the back of his head pretending that Adam Driver was in my chair and coming up with all these fantastic notions, wondering what would happen if the real Adam Driver walked into my shop one day and sat down in my chair for a haircut. I knew, I thought to myself, exactly

*what I'd do and say. I'd tell him I wrote a film treatment—
a synopsis to a film sequel of 'Paterson', the Jim Jarmusch
film he starred in. That I thought a sequel would be a great
idea and that I've flushed out a cool storyline about what
happened to Paterson and Laura in the months and years
after the story of the original film. I would tell him that I've
even envisioned the sequel as a musical, with Broadway-
style showtunes like in the 1950s-era Hollywood musicals
like 'Pal Joey', 'The Pajama Game' and 'South Pacific'. In
my daydream, I spun Adam Driver around and told him if
he liked the idea, I could write the entire screenplay, that I
studied playwriting in college, that my actual university
degree was in dramatic writing, that I've written a dozen
plays, that if I wrote a screenplay and he liked it, he could
bring it to Jim Jarmusch who could direct the sequel; that he
could call Golshifteh Farahani and Barry Shabaka Henley
and William Jackson Harper and Chasten Harmon and
Rizwan Manji who could all reprise their original roles in
my sequel. No sooner did I realize it was Michael that I had
spun around that I smiled and powdered his nape and
forehead and flung the cape from him ending his haircut
service for the evening…and my fanciful daydream…The
idea of the sequel was that Paterson and Laura break up
and eventually divorce, going their separate ways. Paterson
is appointed, first, Poet Laureate of the state of New Jersey
and then of the United States; he moves to Maryland or
Virginia or somewhere near there. Laura's cupcake business
takes off and with a steady stream of income from the three
shops she opened in malls in Paramus and Wayne, New
Jersey and West Nyack, New York, she took off for Nashville
to pursue her dream of becoming a country singer. In
Nashville, she meets all the right people, records a series of
demos and lands a record deal. Her first album, 'Harlequin',*

named after the model of acoustic guitar Paterson bought for her as a present, is an overnight success and her debut single, 'Long Way From Home', makes it to number five on Billboard's Hot Country Songs chart.

As Henny plays the intro to the song, Charlie gets back to work on my haircut and I can tell, though he's performed this song dozens of times by now, that it still chokes him up even after having written the song nearly forty years ago…

While I wrote this song in 1985 as part of the original sad-story breakup musical I was trying to write, I thought it would be the right song for Laura to sing in the sequel. In an imaged scene of the film, Laura is alone in the studio working on a new song for her debut album when she picks up the phone having decided to call Paterson and ask him if he would meet her in Nashville to talk, but she quickly puts down the phone and, with tears in her eyes, picks up her guitar and starts playing the song she'd been working on…

> *They say home is where the heart is*
> *Where you lay your hat that's where home is*
> *Where your name's on the door is where home is*
> *Where there's always room for one more that's*
> *where home is*
>
> *Though we're miles away*
> *We'll be home someday*
>
> *We're a long way from home*
> *A long way from home*
> *We're a long way from home*
> *But we're home*

Leave a light burn in the window for me
I'll be home just as soon as I'm able to be
If I don't return well remember me then
And speak well of me every now and again

Though we're miles away
We'll be home someday

We're a long way from home
A long way from home
We're a long way from home
But we're home

Great falls kiss the clouds up above
Loving arms embrace those below
Where mill town charm would never do you harm
And poetry and laughter overflow

So, leave a light burn in the window for me
I'll be home just as soon as I'm able to be
If I don't return well remember me then
And speak well of me every now and again

Though we're miles away
We'll be home someday

We're a long way from home...

Laura eventually opens her flagship Cupcake Queen boutique in downtown Nashville, selling cupcakes and original clothing and home decor that soon becomes the talk of the town. Soon after, at the back of the shop, she opens Marvin's, a dog delicatessen, café and spa where the Nashville elite bring their dogs for birthday parties, grooming and Laura-designed doggie sweaters, raincoats and accessories. But before long, both Paterson and Laura find their newfound lives and success unfulfilling without each other and coincidentally run into each other at their house in Paterson, which they've recently put on the market. They each made trips back to New Jersey to pack up the rest of their things but, having confused the agreed upon weekend, coincide at the house. They reminisce and talk about the new direction their lives have taken. They decide to spend the weekend together at the house, sleeping in separate rooms. Laura insists on sleeping on the couch in the basement where Paterson used to write his poems, saying she would get up early and start packing things up, not wanting to wake Paterson so early after his five-hour drive from D.C. Before settling in on the couch, Laura sits at the desk where Paterson used to write his poems, looking nostalgically at the jars where he kept various nails, screws, old foreign coins and whatnot; then she opened a drawer to find old copies of 'National Geographic' and 'MAD Magazine'. She smiled as she removed a copy of 'MAD' that had a drawing of the magazine's mascot Alfred E. Neuman on the cover, saying out loud to herself how she never realized how much her ex-husband—how much Paterson— resembled, albeit in a cartoon character way, the magazine's elephantine-eared, tousle-haired, freckle-faced mascot. Just as she went to open the magazine, a few dozen sheets of paper fell out from between its covers and she realized the guts of the magazine had been removed to hold these sheets that, upon closer inspection, were double-sided copies of (could it really be) the poems that were in

Paterson's secret notebook that he was supposed to have made copies of and didn't (did he?) the same day Marvin chewed up the notebook, ripping it to shreds destroying all its contents. So, he did make copies of the poems after all, Laura said to herself out loud in utter disbelief at what she was holding in her hands. He made copies and didn't say a thing, not even when Marvin destroyed the notebook and he seemed so distraught. Laura put the papers back between the magazine covers and returned it to the drawer. She went back over to the couch, got under the blankets and turned out the light, but neither the darkness nor the silence of the cold basement could keep her soft whimpers quiet or her tears from glinting in the reflection of the streetlamp's glow as it shone in from the road outside. The next morning, Laura and Paterson had breakfast together though they barely exchanged a word and spent all day Sunday packing boxes, cleaning and, in the evening, separately meeting friends for dinner in town. On Monday morning, Laura had a meeting with the regional director of Cupcake Queen at eleven at the mall in Paramus, and Paterson thought about walking over to the bus depot to say hello to Donny and his former colleagues or perhaps pick up a coffee at the Burger King on Spruce and Market Streets and walk by the falls and sit on his favorite bench. But he decided to stay at the house and pack up the remaining boxes of tools and supplies (and magazines?) from the basement and garage before heading back to D.C. that afternoon…Paterson was loading the last few boxes into his car when Laura pulled into the driveway. She walked over to him and asked if he needed any help. He thanked her saying those were the last boxes and that he'd be on his way soon. Laura told Paterson that they might be seeing each other again soon as she had just signed off on a new franchise in the Washington, D.C. area and said he'd be welcome to attend the big grand opening in a few months' time. She also invited him to her concert at the Atlantis in D.C. later that year where she was on the bill with Chicago-based record label Bloodshot Records' artists Lydia Loveless and Robbie Fulks. As Paterson drove off, Laura stood in front of the house they shared, wondering if she'd ever really see him again. She felt guilty and responsible for their break up; she was too ambitious and too heartbroken when her parents were tragically killed by a drunk driver on their way from Paterson to their home in Scranton, Pennsylvania, leaving their only child a generous inheritance from the dental practice they ran for nearly forty years. Laura quickly invested the money in her cupcake business and in the months that followed was consumed by grief and obsessed with growing her business, working sometimes twelve to fifteen hours a day with the small staff of bakers getting things ready for the opening while meeting with lawyers, accountants, builders and a slew of hired hands that would get her first three shops open in a matter of months. And all that time, neglecting her relationship and her marriage, too busy to come home for dinners, too preoccupied with her new life that she let her old life simply slip away. Then the move to Nashville and spending more time and money on recording demos, buying clothes and musical instruments, taking voice and guitar lessons; all these things kept her busy and her mind off of the heartbreaking reality of what she left behind back home. And while things were looking up, she had lost the three people who mattered to her and who she loved the most.

And that was how Charlie opened the show; a few stories and a couple of songs that would set up the rest of the performance and engage the audience who, from my ideal vantage point of being sat in the barber chair at center stage looking out directly at them, showed in the expressions on their collective faces that they knew they were taking part in something special, a unique musical theater experience unlike anything they'd ever seen and perhaps would ever see again. Charlie continued by telling the rest of the story of the sequel which, I don't know if I mentioned it before, he titled *A Return to Paterson*. The show, which started out with a sixty-minute runtime, was now, with the addition of a sixth song and a few more anecdotes, just under 75 minutes, but I think the audience would have sat through seventy more.

Opening night was a huge success and Charlie was given a five-minute standing ovation and, breaking with theatrical protocol, he stayed on stage after the applause died down and addressed the audience with a short, unrehearsed speech, thanking them for making it one of the most memorable nights of his life and being a part of his dream come true of performing a one-man show in New York City at a venue that, as he put it, had as much heart and soul as any Broadway or London West End theater. And for that, the audience rose again as Charlie stood there with tears in his eyes as applause rained down on him like a springtime shower. Charlie's moment had arrived.

Saturday night's performance was every bit as good as Friday's and Charlie was visibly more at ease. He had spent the day alone with K., wandering around Midtown, walking to the Central Park Zoo and then back down Park Avenue to the hotel, where they grabbed sandwiches and chips and relaxed in the hotel's cozy canteen before going up to their room for a rest. Charlie's normal twenty-minute power nap lasted nearly an hour, but he woke up

118

refreshed and looked over at K. who was working on her laptop. Seeing Charlie was awake, she jumped onto the bed and playfully hit him over the head with a pillow, then snuggled up with him under the blankets as they looked out high above West 50th Street sharing a moment neither of them could have ever imagined just a few short years earlier. They walked over to theater for the six o'clock call and met Henny and Abbott who were already in the dressing room talking and sharing a beer and a bowl of guacamole with tortilla chips. Charlie and Henny then walked onto the stage to do some vocal warmups and go over the running order of the show, which Charlie had made two changes in by swapping out two stories for alternates, something Charlie did regularly to make each performance unique and keep things feeling spontaneous and fresh from show to show. Once again, as Charlie curiously looked on, and just like on opening night the evening before, two house crew members brought out a few additional chairs and placed them at the front of the house, telling Charlie the theater manager had requested the extra chairs so that she and her sisters could see tonight's performance. *The more the merrier*, Charlie said to the two young men who replied with thumbs up and toothy grins.

After the opening number, rather than going into the Café Society stories of his 80s new wave band as he often did at this juncture of the performance, Charlie explained, like he always did early in the show, how he came to writing a screenplay for a sequel to his favorite film. But then, he began talking about the contrasts between three of Adam Driver's film characters—Charlie Barber in *Marriage Story*, Phillip Altman in *This is Where I Leave You* and Henry McHenry in *Annette*—all who suffered failed romantic relationships, which Charlie compared and contrasted to his own three failed relationships. What a departure, I thought to myself, never having heard this particular story before. I sat and listened as attentively as ever...

The more I delved deeper into Adam Driver's filmography, the more I kept discovering similarities in some of the roles he played as the stories of these characters—three specifically—resonated with stories of my own; to be more concrete, stories of the three major breakups I'd experienced in my life. One of Driver's characters was going through a divorce (Charlie Barber), one was in a new relationship that quickly came apart at the seams by the time the film ended (Phillip Altman) and one had gone through the transformations of being in a relationship, getting married to that person and then losing her in a tragic event (Henry McHenry). I met my ex-wife in Granada, Spain in December of 1991. Virginia had just graduated from the University of Granada with a degree in biology and was getting ready to go back home to Alicante to start the next chapter of her life (funny, after all these years I never knew what her plans actually were). I had flown to Spain for the holidays after having finished my first quarter at university and Virginia and I were introduced by a mutual friend (who I'm still in touch with today). A month later, I found myself at O'Hare International Airport in Chicago, picking Virginia up—on her 24th birthday, of all days—as she had decided that moving in with me just a month after we'd met would be the next chapter of her life. We were married on April 1st 1992 (yes, I know, April Fool's Day, right?) and lived in Chicago until the summer of 1996, when Virginia accepted a job and the opportunity to finish her Ph.D. at the

University of Valencia School of Medicine in Spain. Our son was born the following year and our daughter, twenty months later. Challenges notwithstanding, I loved being married—being married to Virginia; she was smart, beautiful and caring and everything a man could ever hope for in a wife and mother. But we made the fatal mistake of starting a business together (a translation service) which, by 2003, was taking its toll on our marriage, as we had an ever-increasing rift in the way we thought the business should be run. And on the day she returned from her parents' house in Alicante after having spent a week there putting the finishing touches on her doctoral dissertation, we stood in the kitchen of the apartment we had recently purchased and completely renovated from top to bottom, when she told me our relationship was beyond repair. That same day, she took our children to live in the nearby apartment we had lived in for the past five years (we were waiting out the last months of our lease and still living there as our new home was being renovated) and that was the end of our marriage. Like Charlie and Nicole in 'Marriage Story'—though not as tumultuous—our divorce was long, drawn out and extremely painful for everyone involved. Meetings with lawyers and accountants and realtors and prospective buyers (we decided to put our apartment up for sale after only having lived there as a family for less than six months) began to take their toll and I spiraled into depression, eventually losing my advertising sales job, my company and, if I'm to be honest here, my will to carry on. And all through this, I was still the primary caregiver to our children who—only six and four at the time—were probably suffering as much as anyone. It took nearly three years for our divorce to become finalized. We met at the courthouse with our respective lawyers, waited (forever it seemed, pacing the *corridors), and when we were called, went into a small office and sat behind the small desk of the small judge, signed some papers and that was that. Charlie and Nicole were a marriage story no more...*

A few months later, on the day of my forty-third birthday at some event at the synagogue, I finally got up the courage to ask Natalia out on a date. She emphatically, though politely, declined. Natalia had lived in Valencia for about a year, where she worked as a home caregiver to the elderly while going through the demanding process of converting to Judaism. I had seen her in shul many times but never had the nerve to approach her. I was already in my forties, probably ten years older than her, divorced and with two young children and fairly certain this stunningly gorgeous, olive-skinned, burnt-umber-haired, black-eyed Spanish woman would be uninterested in me. But on that particular Sunday afternoon, at the event at shul, I turned, innocently enough, to Natalia and asked her if she would accompany the kids and me over the grocers to buy a few more bottles of Coke and Fanta, as the supplies were dwindling. She agreed and in the ten or so minutes we were gone, I noticed Natalia looking pensively at my children, smiling and even holding my daughter's hand at the street crossing. At the end of the afternoon, I approached Natalia, thanking her again for coming with us to buy the sodas and asking if she needed a ride home, telling her I would be more than happy to drop her off. She kindly accepted my offer and I drove her to the apartment where she was renting a room from a spinster (I know we don't say spinster anymore, but I love the word and actually find it endearing). Anyway, I got out of the car and walked around to the passenger-side door, opened it and accompanied Natalia to the door of the apartment building. She thanked me and rang the bell, the door soon buzzing open. 'Can I see you sometime?' I asked, holding the door open as she was walking in through the doorway. 'You're very sweet and your children are lovely,' Natalia said. 'But it's probably best not to'. Over the next few weeks, I would drive Natalia home after Friday night services, where we exchanged niceties and small conversation. On the evenings where the kids hadn't joined me, Natalia and I would sit for a few minutes, sometimes longer, in the car outside of her building talking about this and that, becoming more and more comfortable in each other's company. I don't remember exactly why, it certainly didn't have any overtly romantic connotations, but one day she gave me her phone number and later that week, after having looked at that phone number a hundred times, I decided to conjure up some stupid excuse to call her. And I did…We spoke on the phone a few times and one day, out of the blue (and to my surprise), she called me. She told me she had just taken a new job caring for an elderly woman near the maritime district and didn't finish her shift until eleven, and asked if I would be interested, and available, to pick her up after work and bring her home, and that she would pay me for my trouble. I told her I would do it, but I wouldn't accept any money; and when she insisted, I told her to donate the money, put it in her 'tzedakah' box before Shabbos every Friday night. She loved that I asked her to do that and I think it was that small gesture that finally won her over. One night, I drove over to where Natalia lived and called her from the street below her house. She answered and I told her to look out of her window at the bench on the sidewalk at the top of the street. She waved from the window and hung up the phone and a few minutes later joined me on the bench. But there was something wrong, a look on her face I knew concealed something I didn't even want to imagine. She told me how much she appreciated my friendship and loved spending time with me, but that she couldn't see me again, not as friends, not as her trusted driver, not as anything. I couldn't for the life of me understand why; what could I have done or said to provoke this, I wondered. Then she confessed and what she told me was utterly devastating…Like her mother and grandmother before her, Natalia had been diagnosed, from an early age, with Schizophrenia, and it was severe. She had been in and out of psychiatric hospitals and therapy and on medication for years which, she said, had horrible side effects and she often discontinued her treatments going against her doctor's explicit instructions not to. She told me she was falling in love with me—and my children—and that was her reason for telling me she could no longer see me and the reason she had decided to return to Alicante and live with her parents as she had done nearly all her life. Did she just say she was falling in love with me? I must have hallucinated that part, but no, she really said it, and more than just saying it, she said it with so much…I don't know, it's hard to put into words, but she said it with so much intensity that the words reverberated deep within me. And in the same breath that she told me she was falling in love with me, she said she could no longer see me, ever again, and that she was leaving Valencia and moving away. We got off of the bench and, silently without as much as exchanging a glance, I walked her home and she disappeared into the stairwell as I stood in the doorway heartbroken. I fought off the urge to call her as soon as I got home, but I thought by giving her some space would be the better choice. I went into the kitchen and warmed up some sweet and sour cabbage soup (my great-grandmother's old-world recipe) I had made the day before and no sooner did I sit down at the table, my phone rang. It was Natalia. And she wanted to see me, perhaps as soon as tomorrow. I met Natalia at a café on the Gran Vía, near her house, one she said she frequented regularly so 'we'd be safe there'. We sat outside and I drank tomato juice while Natalia sipped black iced coffee with a slice of lemon placed on the rim of the glass. I never really had the chance to look at her in the direct sunlight as we'd often met indoors or in the evening and what the daylight revealed was the most beautiful woman I'd ever seen. She had flawless skin and a perfect mouth, lips not too thin nor excessively plump, though divinely sensual and I couldn't help thinking what kissing them would feel like. Her eyes, ears, nose, cheekbones and chin were perfect, like a painting or sculpture that highlighted every immaculate detail. Her neck was long and the wispy hairs that adorned her nape made me yearn to press my lips to the base of her throat and slowly move towards her ears leaving gentle kisses along the journey to her neck. Then, the sound of a spoon falling to the ground stirred me from my sensual daydream and Natalia looked at me and said, 'the woman on the right heard everything you were thinking and dropped that spoon on purpose to break the spell'. What was she talking about? I asked myself. What woman? Heard what I was thinking?? Dropped the spoon on purpose??? 'I can tell when people are talking about me; or thinking about me,' Natalia said in a calm and matter-of-fact way. 'That's why I have to move out of the house where I'm living, the people across the patio are talking about me night and day and I can't take much more. And then there are the white pigeons…' I was at a loss for words and before I had a chance to speak, Natalia took my hand and said, 'I will come to live with you, but it won't last. I will be the greatest love of your life, but it won't last. And we will be happy together for a time, but it won't last, and when it ends, it will bring you the greatest sadness that has ever overcome you heart, one that will endure until the day you die. But I will love you and love your children with all my heart and if Hashem wills it, you will never regret being with me whether it lasts a day a week a year or a lifetime.'

Later that day, I drove back to Natalia's house and called her from the car. A few minutes later, she walked out of the building for the last time carrying a brown leather duffle and two plastic carrier bags from Mercadona that appeared to be filled with clothes and shoes. I got out of the car, opened the hatch and helped Natalia put her things inside. I walked around and opened the passenger door and Natalia got in. As I drove away, Natalia pointed to a small park at the end of the street and asked me to pull over. She pointed at a park bench and said, 'I used to sit on that bench for hours studying Torah and smoking like a loca. I quit last year, smoking, and still study the Torah, but in private, on my own, when I know I'm really alone, when it's only Hashem and me'. Then she turned up the volume on the cassette player (which was playing a song from James Iha's 1998 solo album, 'Let it Come Down'), pulled me towards her and kissed me until the very last note of the four-minute and twelve-second song faded into silence...

'No one's gonna hurt you, not anymore; Ever since I've met you I've come to adore you; And I know they've hurt you bruised and sore; And I want to love you a nightingale that longs to sleep and sound; No one's gonna hurt you, no one's gonna hurt you not anymore; If I hold you close I will take you to a secret world where no one knows...'

Natalia and I lived together for the next nine months and I'm quite guarded when it comes to sharing details about that time as it was as blissful and as tempestuous as any time I have spent living with anyone. But when bliss meets the tempest, the storm it can produce can be equally as wonderful as they can be destructive and consuming. But Natalia was right about one thing, hers was the greatest love I'd ever known up until that point in my life. And just like the tempest in the film 'Annette', where Adam Driver played the tormented and agitational stand-up comedian Henry McHenry, the storm in the film was the turning point which drove him to the brink and would forever change his life and the life of those nearest and dearest to him. Natalia drove me to the brink and when the storm clouds finally parted and the sun shone through, she was gone in the blink of an eye and, even after all these years, whenever storm clouds gather and lightning strikes and thunder bellows, I hear Natalia's voice calling to me in the gale whispering softly, 'it will never last'.

Every night of the New York run, a pall of melancholy fell over the audience at the end of that monologue and the mélange of Charlie's words and emotions were palpable. For some reason, Saturday night's performance—this part of the show anyway—was particularly poignant. Not that the other performances or deliveries were not, there was something different in Charlie that night. In the dressing room after the show as I was removing the light layer of makeup from my face, I wanted so badly to ask Charlie about it, but at once he was animated and in the highest spirits I'd seen him in so far that weekend, so I let it go, thinking to myself how difficult it must be for him to relive these stories every night, singing these songs written mostly as he anguished over the past and the loves he had and lost. And as much as I admired Charlie for his talent and gifts and the amazing life he has had—maybe to the point of envy—I didn't envy the obvious pain he must have endured to be able to recount, night after night, the hardships, loss and yearning he expressed in his performances. And as the show wound down, Charlie gave the last example of what he called *Adam Driver's trilogy of lovelorn characters* in his recounting of the last long-term relationship he had before meeting K…

You would think of all the characters Adam Driver portrayed, Phillip Altman in Shawn Levy's 2016 'This Is Where I Leave You', should be considered the most footloose and fancy free. After all, he's self-made (well, at least in fits and starts), and when we meet him after his father's funeral while the family sits shiva in the Altman's home in the upscale Long Island village of Munsey Park, New York, he tells one visitor that he runs an alternative fuel think-tank in Washington, D.C., while a few minutes later tells another guest he's running a small private equity fund. And he's engaged ('engaged to be engaged', as she put it) to his (former) therapist who is fifteen years older and well enough to do that she gifts her 'loverboyfriend' a two-hundred-thousand-dollar Porsche 911 Carrera S Cabrio. But in the short time she is at Phillip's family home, his lady friend sees a side of her boyfriend that she apparently never saw (in therapy or otherwise), that he was still an immature, philandering man-child and, by the time the film gets to the one hour and twenty-six-minute mark, she breaks up with him, takes her suitcase and gets into a taxi never, we assume, to see Phillip again…So, you may be wondering, what do Phillip Altman and I have in common? Well, though it stings to say it, the immature man-child part seems to hit close to home, seems to fit the bill—and I'm not saying it in a self-deprecating way—I mean, I have issues (we all have issues). Now this is neither the time or the place to go into all the particulars, but let me summarize it the best way I can…One: abandonment issues. My biological father left my mother and me when I was a baby and to be honest, I don't know if he was even there at all. I'd heard stories that the day I was born he had a sedan full of high school cheerleaders waiting outside of Louis A. Weiss Memorial Hospital on Marine Drive for him. Well, maybe that's a bit exaggerated, but there was a sedan (an expensive sedan his wealthy father bought for him in exchange for his promise to not enlist in the army); and there was a girl (maybe two) in said sedan. He was the philandering part of Phillip Altman that I never was. Two: Hypochondriasis, neurosis and borderline personality disorder. Personally, I like the alternative version of 'emotionally unstable personality disorder'. That one has a bit of extra kick, don't you think? Here's the lowdown: I notice a lump, it's cancer. It's a zit. Feeling a bit tired. Leukemia. It's because I'm tired. Stomach ache. Cancer. It's nerves. So, I worry. Neurosis? In 1798, some French guy came up with these four categories of neurosis: melancholia (I got that one big time); mania (if we're talking about excessive enthusiasm or obsession, I guess I'm in); dementia (no); idiotism (uh uh)…Next. The borderline thing? I don't buy it. Nobody's perfect, they just happen to have a name for my particular brand of imperfection. Three: Peter Pan Syndrome. Is it a real thing? Well, not really, not medically anyway. It's a metaphor (not contagious!). So, am I trapped in my childhood? Maybe. Don't want to grow up? Seriously? You see all the problems grown-ups get into. No thanks…So, this Phillip Altman role of Driver's? Sure, I can relate. His girlfriend was smart enough in the end to give him up, but my Phillip Altman's girlfriend in my Phillip Altman world waited until she sucked every last bit of life out of me until she spit me out.

I never thought I'd come to know anyone so diabolical or alone spend a mostly miserable fifteen years of my life with that person. But that's what happens when a child—or a man who never really ever grew up—is swept off his feet by a Dr. Jekyll/Mr. Hyde narcissist psychopath and master manipulator without an ounce of empathy who used me first as rebound from her failed marriage and then as a sperm donor (three times!) until our daughters were old enough and she figured she could just easily discard me and endeavored to make my life a living hell of abuse, endlessly talking down to, criticizing, bullying and belittling me, neglecting me (I was eventually relinquished to a single bed in the doorless downstairs office) and gaslighting (she would contradict stories I knew to be accurate, flip the cutlery upside down in the drawer, move the dirty laundry hamper so the shower door would always bump into it and hang the cutting knives in the opposite direction to the way I hung them, to name of few of her favorite hobbies). I don't feel it's worth the time or effort or of any value to burden you with any of the other details about this mean-spirited, conniving, two-faced, clothes hoarding, disloyal, sloppy, lazy, unsupportive woman—

Let me quickly summarize… We met in Valencia while we were both married to Spaniards, who we later divorced. We worked together in a school (she dreaded the idea of my being hired and tried unsuccessfully to thwart that). She moved away and returned to Spain a few years later and we reconnected, discovering we had each divorced our Spanish spouses. By this time, the pall known as the economic crisis of 2007 had fallen over Spain and what was left of my savings and small business ventures had been sucked into the black hole of Spain's economic downturn. She was fed up with Spain and the low wages and lack of a clear career path so she got a job in England. As for me, I was recently divorced, had two kids and just ended a serious relationship, so I was pretty much defeated without a lot of options or motivation. So, to make a long story short, I followed along. We settled down in Liverpool, where she worked at a university and I taught Spanish to school-aged kids at a Catholic primary school. I also wrote some articles for the 'Jewish Chronicle' and did stand-up comedy (if you can believe that). Our first daughter was born twelve months after we arrived in Liverpool, and I was back to being a full-time stay-at-home father which, it seems, is the only job I've ever really been any good at, actually enjoyed and never got fired from. After her contract ended, we moved to the Netherlands (Holland, for all those who are shrugging their shoulders); we both worked as teachers (though she parlayed her teaching job into a nearly six-figure administrative position), had two more daughters and lived miserably ever after. But I don't want to dwell on that for too long.

*But where
that horror story ends, a new and truly beautiful story
begins. And now, K. has made me the happiest man in the
world. Her gentle kindness, her infinite patience and the
serene and mindful way she lives her life changed mine. And
that's what inspired me to really go out there and explore
the crazy idea I had about writing the sequel to a movie that
my only relationship to was as a spectator and fan. But, yet,
in the film 'Paterson', there was something hidden behind
what looked like the perfect marriage—the ideal
relationship—that just didn't sit well with me. I knew that
Paterson and Laura wouldn't last, not the way they were,
not with so many unfulfilled desires that the other could
have never fully comprehended or, in some ways, become a
part of.*

At that point in the performance, Charlie takes the longest
pause of the entire show—nearly a minute—which in stage
time can feel like an awkward eternity. But that was
Charlie's intention, to add a little tension to the stew, to

make people feel just slightly on edge. And it worked. Soon enough, Henny began to play and Charlie sings a song about how sometimes being lost is the only way of *finding* your way...

> *There's a sun above me*
> *And it's shining in my weary eyes*
> *While the clouds surround me*
> *It seems they're not the ones I used to see*
> *Casting shadows wantonly*
> *That slowly fall around me*
>
> *There's a new day dawning*
> *And it's right before my very eyes*
> *At the break of morning*
> *I see I'm not the man I used to be*
> *My soul's adrift in a sea of lonely longing*
> *Not belonging*
>
> *Missing you*
> *Missing kissing you*
> *Missing the bliss you brought into my life*
> *Wishing you*
> *I've been wishing you*
> *Wishing you were still my wife*
>
> *Now the road I've traveled*
> *Has taken me so far and wide*
> *Over land and water*
> *But it's by your side I want to be*
> *The journey's long and hopelessly*
> *I need to be beside you*

In the final hour
The sun sets and the birds fly south
Like the blooming flower
Its petals blow into the wind
Branches break and saplings bend
I'm lost then I am found again

Missing you
Missing kissing you
Missing the bliss you brought into my life
Wishing you
I've been wishing you
Wishing you were still my wife

Wishing to
I've been wishing to
Hold you in my arms and not let go
And if I do, I will see this through
And spend the rest of my life loving you

Saturday night's afterparty was an absolute gasser. Unbeknownst to anyone (except for K., I imagine), Charlie rented out a small room in the theater complex where a lavish buffet table, open bar and deejay booth were set up. Charlie invited the entire crew and some friends that had come to that evening's performance to enjoy some good food, drink and music. Upon closer inspection, while the attractive Asian woman at the buffet table appeared to be a sushi chef in her dress and demeanor, I didn't actually see a single fish in sight. It turned out Charlie hired Sayuri Oyamada, a Japanese actress and model who, during an existential crisis during the COVID-19 pandemic (sound familiar?), started making rice balls and sushi rolls in New York, only to have her concept take off and become one of the city's most sought-after vegan caterers. And of course, there was a twist at the bar as well. A tuxedoed barman Liam Durow, who hailed from Durban, South Africa and had been living in New York for the past ten years as the quintessential struggling actor, started his Movers & Shakers traveling bar business two years earlier and had become, so to speak, the toast of the town who now employed forty bartenders, owned four mobile bars and was booked for two years in advance by wedding and event planners from Buffalo to the Bronx. But there was no booze in Liam's bottles this night as what he was moving and shaking were the funkiest mocktails one could imagine, packed with exotic flavors, fresh fruit juices and creamy concoctions unlike anything I'd ever tried. And the finishing touch was an amazing mix of music that wasn't too loud or overbearing that covered a wide range of genres from Chet Baker and The Beatles to Fetty Wap and Ennio Morricone. The party broke up just after midnight and Charlie was one of the first to leave, shaking hands and hugging everyone present saying that he needed his beauty sleep in anticipation of Sunday's doubleheader and the closing of his brief theatrical escapade in New York. I stayed around finishing up the last few drops of my drink and talking to Abbott about his life in Zurich and listening to his recollections about Charlie as a first-year college student. I made it back to my hotel and called home to say goodnight to my wife and daughters before turning in, exhausted but filled with a sense of gladness and delight and ever so grateful for Charlie having made me a part of all this. As I was falling asleep, I imagined what tomorrow would bring and what would happen after that and where things could possibly go from here. I'd find out soon enough, but there was still Sunday and it couldn't come fast enough.

Brunch was at ten-thirty at Friedman's, which was packed and buzzing with what I imagined was the regular Sunday crowd. The sounds of cutlery tinkling on porcelain, the rumble bellowing from inside the kitchen and conversations in a babel of foreign tongues and dialects made the scene electric but in a subdued and familiar way, like Thanksgiving dinner with extended family or a wedding where an almost sublime chaos was congenial and, in sharp contrast, surprisingly calm. Charlie arrived and looked well-rested. He greeted everyone and sat down next to Henny as K. walked around to the other side of the table and sat next to Henny's wife, with whom she had become even closer to during these past few days.

We arrived at the theater for our twelve-thirty call and it felt as if we'd been doing it for ages. I wonder what the 1953 cast of *Guys and Dolls* must have thought on the last day of their twelve-hundred-show run, one thousand one hundred days after opening at the now Richard Rodgers Theatre on West 46th Street. While I was looking forward to getting back to the Netherlands, back to my family and familiar routines, part of me wished this could go on forever. And while I was just a supporting character in this play (both onstage and off), it may have been one of the most exciting things I'd ever experienced and I was sad to think about losing that exhilarating feeling. One surprising thing out of all the surprising things that had occurred up until this point of the weekend, was Charlie's not mentioning anything about Adam Driver. I couldn't be sure if it was because he didn't want to raise his expectations (he knew Driver coming to see the show was a long shot, but held out hope) or if he had been so caught up in the splendor of it all, he merely put it out of his mind. And just like before the previous performances, like clockwork, there were the stagehands, each with a single folding chair under their arm. But this time, they each walked around to different sides of the theater, one setting his chair down in a small recess next to the third row, while the other man set his chair at the very back of the house closest to the door. Hmm, I thought, a chair for someone who perhaps didn't want to attract a lot of attention to themselves and who, seeing the close proximity of the chair to the door, could make a quick getaway once the final curtain fell.

The matinee crowd was very different from the previous nights' audiences, somewhat younger—students? young executives?? I thought to myself—more casually dressed in jeans and blazers, skirts and cardigans. But who was sitting in that chair in the back row? Not that the stage lights were blindingly bright, they were fairly subdued, as Charlie wanted to make sure he could maintain visual contact with the audience. But I still couldn't make out the lone figure at the back of house. It was definitely a man, and he certainly looked tall, lanky even. But maybe it was just my imagination playing tricks on me because, just as much as Charlie, I was praying that Adam Driver would show up just as Charlie had imagined it when this whole crazy train took off from the station back in The Hague in what seemed like a long time ago.

Charlie's performance was stellar and the audience responded in kind with another long-standing ovation. But as the house lights came up and I looked for the figure who had been sitting in the lone folding chair, the man was gone and nowhere to be seen. Stranger still, the chair gone as well! Later, as the stagehands were making their rounds, I stopped them and asked if they knew who was sitting in the folding chair at the back and what happened to the chair. They said his name was Boris, that he'd been coming to shows there for years. "Rumors had it," they added, "he was some philanthropist or patron of the arts and went to just about every show in town, Broadway, off-Broadway, off-off Broadway and supported a number of local theaters and theater companies with generous donations, most of them anonymous. And he always sits on a folding chair at the back and takes his chair out following every performance," they added.

So, it wasn't Adam Driver and there was only one more show to go. But, I wondered, what if Driver had already been there? What if he already saw the show and slipped in and out unnoticed (which would kind of be a challenge for a famous movie star who stands at six foot three!). Anything is possible, I suppose, but I feel it was pretty unlikely that Driver could have been there and no one saw him. It all came down to the final performance, one last chance for Charlie's dream to come to fruition, one more show and I would do anything to see Adam Driver replace me in the barber chair on stage. We had a three-hour break before our next call and we all headed our separate ways. Charlie called me just as I was walking into the elevator at my hotel to ask me if I was okay and if there was anything I needed before tonight's show. How odd, I thought to myself. What could I have needed? Was I okay?? We were together about fifteen minutes ago laughing about the woman who sneezed during the performance only to have Charlie respond *gezundeheyt* in his best Yiddish accent (which brought cackles from nearly everyone in the house!). Something was strange about that call, but I didn't pay much mind to it. "Bring me a French Cruller from Dunkin,'" I said. "And, I'm fine, very fine," I added. Back in my room I must have dozed off as I was awakened by a text message ping. It was K. asking if I was with Charlie. Odd, I thought, so I called her and asked what was up. K. said that Charlie never made it back to the hotel, that he said he needed to do a couple of things and he'd be right along. But she said that was more than an hour ago and Charlie wasn't picking up his phone and no one had seen him at the theater. I told her he may have gone over to Dunkin' Donuts and that I would run over there and see. K. told me she was actually there herself as she had overheard our conversation earlier. I told K. not to worry and that he probably just went for a stroll to get some fresh air and psyche himself up for closing night. She agreed and I told her I'd see her at the theater.

At the five o'clock call, Charlie was nowhere to be found and phone calls went straight to voice mail. Now, I'm not the worrying type, but I have to admit I was a bit concerned as it wasn't like Charlie to drop off the radar and be incommunicado. Just then, K. appeared holding Charlie's backpack in one hand and his cellphone in the other and a look of worry on her face. He had apparently left these in his dressing room and no one in the building had seen him come or go. And before we could say another word, Charlie and Henny walked into theater and K.'s sigh of relief reverberated across the room.

"We were worried about you. You left without your phone," K. said.

"I did?" replied Charlie as he reached into the chest pocket of his jacket surprised to find it missing. "I did, indeed," he said. "I never do that."

"It must be all the excitement," K. added. "But where did you disappear to for three hours?"

It turned out that as they were leaving the theater complex, Charlie and Henny were talking about their common family origins and how Charlie's Ashkenazi ancestors fled modern-day Ukraine to avoid religious persecution in the early 1900s. All at once, Charlie was overcome by a sudden urge and hailed a yellow cab and he and Henny drove off to Battery Park and boarded the ferry to Ellis Island. As the Statue of Liberty came into view, both men looked at each other and nodded their heads wistfully. Charlie's maternal great-grandparents, grandmother and great-uncle, as well as his paternal great-grandfather, all arrived in the United States at Ellis Island. His biological father's grandfather, Jacob Sandman, arrived from Bremen, Germany, on the *Kronprinz Wilhelm*, on December 11th 1906 at the age of eighteen. His maternal family arrived from Cherbourg, France, on the *RMS Aquitania* on September 7th 1923 (there's that number 23 again!). They all settled in Chicago—mostly on the West Side—where members of their respective families had gone upon their arrivals to America. Charlie and Henny sat on a bench outside of the Great Hall, talking about the plights of their families, Charlie's, now more than one hundred years prior and Henny's, a matter of only a few short years. They talked and, in between anecdotes, sat reflectively looking at the massive building designed by architects Edward Lippincott Tilton and William Alciphron Boring, whose construction began in 1887, then used as the processing center for arriving immigrants. For Charlie, the experience of visiting Ellis Island for the first time was life-altering, and standing on that hallowed ground where his ancestors once walked as they arrived for processing in the Great Hall was emotionally overwhelming. But he was glad he made the trip and happy to have shared that experience with Henny, but it was getting late and the two headed back to the ferry landing to begin their journey back to the theater where in just a few hours Charlie's dream of putting on his show in New York would—now realized—come to an end, and in the back of his mind he wondered if a special guest would finally show up and change his fortunes.

If there are two things I love about being a barber—and believe me when I tell you there a hundred things I love about being a barber—I'd have to say it's the variety and spontaneity. Now, that's going to need a bit of explanation. I don't mean in the work itself. You know, there's no great mystery to cutting hair and I hate it when people call me an artist or think I do some creative, mystical, magical thing. For me, there's nothing artistic and certainly nothing really creative about cutting hair—okay, so maybe I style your hair in a way that suits you, but tomorrow morning, when you're in front of the mirror with a comb in your hand and styling your own hair, does that make you a barber? Barbers are tradesmen, like electricians, plumbers, masons and mechanics (though ninety-nine per cent of them will never earn the same money as even a journeyman earns in those other trades). I love that every guy that sits in my chair is an island, a universe all unto themselves, possessing a myriad of stories, experiences, worldviews, opinions, thoughts, dreams, fantasies, fears and flaws. And the greatest privilege of being a barber is when, and it happens ever so infrequently, a customer lets down their guard, removes their mask, opens their heart and lets you see their humanity. Now, granted I'm a blabbermouth, there's no disputing that (didya notice?), but I never once go to work thinking about how much blather I'm going to spew that evening. I never throw a story out there at random, that's to say I never—and I mean never—would say to a customer, 'hey, did I ever tell you about that one time, blah, blah, blah'…But, and I say but, if you ask me about something I'll more likely than not give you a fairly protracted answer. And that's how it usually happens. A customer will have read something in my bio on my website and say, 'so, you're from Chicago, the Windy City; must be really windy there'…Well, that's enough to get me going on a tangent. It's not called the Windy City because of the wind (it's actually the eighth windiest city in the United States!)…and then of course I'm obliged to tell them why it's called the Windy City and while I'm visiting that I feel the need to tell them about Chicago's other nicknames—the city of broad shoulders, the third coast, the second city, to name a few—just because if you're going to explain something, you might as well explain it right. That's my thought on the matter anyway…Yeah, it's a great job and I love all the connections, the conversations, the trust that others place in me. And funny thing is, they keep coming back. Okay, so I get it that if you want a haircut on a Monday night at eleven o'clock, I'm literally the only one in town that's open; and let's be honest, I haven't been a barber all that long and feel I'm still learning, still honing the craft, perfecting my skills. There are definitely better barbers in town, but none of those guys work at night, so I guess you could say I cornered the market. I'm not suggesting I'm a bad barber, I'm pretty decent and getting better all the time, but I do think my customers come to me for more than a late-night cut or beard trim and I take pride in treating my customers with respect and dignity and, when it comes their turn to talk, to *lay down whatever it is on their mind that's bringing them up or down, I'd like to think I'm a good listener and hope they feel I am...So, of course I've gone way off track with what I wanted to say about tonight's performance (yeah, so I'm breaking that fourth wall again, I tend to do that every now and then), but something unexpected—and spontaneous—happened today after the matinee. Henny and I—oh, this is Henny (how about a nice round of applause for Henny!)—Henny and I took the ferry to Ellis Island a few hours ago. I'd never been there and Henny had never been there. And we sat outside the Great Hall—the place where my ancestors first set foot on American soil more than a hundred years ago—talking about how much we had in common in that our families have long histories living in what is now Ukraine, though mine fled a century ago and he and his family less than a few years back. My great-grandfather, his wife, daughter—my grandmother— and son, stood in a line, for hours perhaps, waiting to step up to the counter and face the immigration inspector for the first time—we've all seen that in dozens of films right?—like little Vito Andolini stepping up to the counter and the inspector impatiently asks the boy his name while another inspector who is standing there looks at the boy's name tag and says to his colleague, 'he's Vito Andolini from Corleone'; and the inspector, writing in his log says, 'Corleone, Vito Corleone'. So, I imagined my great-grandfather standing before the man with his Polish papers (they spent time in Warsaw before coming to America and their Russian names were transliterated into Polish), the inspector looking at the names on the documents: Owszyja, Rosie, Mania and Jacob Usiatynski and, probably like he'd done a thousand times before, anglicized the names to Samuel, Rose, Mary and Jack. He also conveniently*

removed the 'U' and the 'ski' and their family name became,
in the stroke of a pen, 'Satin'. And as I was telling Henny
that story, my imagination took hold of me and I thought
about the screenplay for the Paterson sequel and the part of
the film where I imagined Paterson standing at the foot of
the Reflecting Pool in front of the Lincoln Monument—in
the same place where Forrest Gump and Jenny are
reunited—on the brink of calling Laura and asking for
another chance, while we see Laura sitting alone in the
recording studio thinking the exact same thing just about to
dial her phone.

And that, to everyone's surprise, was the story Charlie
inserted into the show on closing night right after the
opening number, in a space he usually reserves for stories
about growing up in his grandparents' apartment or his
first trip to Spain (you remember the coin and public
phone story). And then, signaling to Henny to begin
playing, Charlie sung this song…

> *In this great big town*
> *Where I lay my head down*
> *I've got my head in the clouds*
> *And my feet on the ground*
> *In this great big town*
> *Where I lay my head down*
> *I'm missing you*
>
> *You called to ask me how I'm doin'*
> *And I said I'm doin' well*
> *I've been trying to make the best of things*
> *At least as far as I can tell*
>
> *So, I asked you how you've been feelin'*

And you said you've been feelin' fine
Then I wondered if you ever thought of me
At least from time to…

Time and time again I think about
All the things that we'd been through
I never would have had the life I've had
Had it not been for my life with you

The years flew by like a hurricane
A whirlwind of happy days
Then the winds of change came and rearranged
Everything in so many ways

Now I'm here on my own
Waking up alone I'm prone to talking to
No one on the telephone; only a reminder that
I'm merely skin and bone on my own

So, I open up the window and look outside
Wondering where you are
Miles and miles away from anywhere
Doesn't really seem that far

But the time and space between us won't erase
All the things that came to pass
When the future was lost to yesterday
And tomorrow found in the past

Now I'm here on my own
Waking up alone I'm prone to talking to
No one on the telephone; only a reminder that
I'm merely skin and bone on my own

In this great big town
Where I lay my head down
I'm missing you

But before all that happened, I suppose you're wondering about the stagehands and the extra chairs. Well, I guess it won't be any surprise if I tell you they brought out a single chair, again (not sure why they both had to come out, but they did) and, just like before the matinee hours earlier, set the chair in the last row next to the exit. Now, I've never considered myself to be someone with a heightened sense of intuition, but I had a feeling in the pit of my stomach that tonight that chair would be occupied by someone very special and I envisioned seeing the silhouette of Adam Driver walking in just as the lights dimmed, taking a seat in that lone folding chair at the back of the house. And then it happened. I was behind the curtain watching as the door closed and the murmur of the audience began to subside. And, just like my premonition, the door opened as the lights were being dimmed and in walked a tall, lanky figure. This time I had a better vantage point and I thought it was my eyes playing a trick on me, but it looked just like him, albeit in the dark with merely a wisp of light shining over him from behind as the door slowly closed. He waited until closing night, how perfect, I thought. My mind was racing. Would Charlie see him? Should I tell him?? Abbott was the one in charge of scanning the audience and surely he would see him. Then what? Charlie and Abbott had an arrangement that if Adam Driver was to come to the theater, Abbott would tell Henny from the wings and Henny would play the first few notes of "Being Alive" from Sondheim's musical *Company*, the song that Driver's character Charlie Barber sang in the lounge scene in *Marriage Story*. That would cue Charlie that Driver was in the house and what he called his Plan A (for Adam) would go into full tilt. Plan A meant that Driver was in the house and that Charlie would, if all went to plan, walk around from behind his barber chair, whisk the cape off of me, shake my hand as if he was saying goodbye and then address the audience...*Ladies and gentleman, it has come to my attention that a very special walk-in customer appears to be in need of a haircut service this evening. And while I usually enforce a strict appointment-only policy, tonight I will make a rare exception.* And that's how Plan A would come off and Charlie would introduce Driver who would, for better or worse, feel obligated to come up onto the stage and take a seat in Charlie's chair. Then, as he rehearsed it in his mind a thousand times, he'd wet Driver's hair and comb through it (while whispering into his ear that he wasn't going to really cut anything) and begin his spiel...

...And after seeing 'Marriage Story', and seeing how I was homebound due to the lockdown, I started watching as many of your films as I could find. And I tell people I'd never seen you in a film before that but when I checked your filmography on Wikipedia that summer, it said you'd appeared as some Samuel Beckett or Beckwith in Spielberg's 'Lincoln', which I had literally seen (well listened to) over a thousand times as 'Lincoln' was one of the films I used to lull myself to sleep every night by hanging my iPad over the headboard. So, eventually I came across 'Paterson', a film unlike any film I'd ever seen. And to this day, I still can't put my finger on exactly what enthralled me so profoundly about that film, but it did and I was. It's still one of only three films—'Moneyball' and 'The Judge' being the other two—that I use nightly as sleeping pills, so to speak. So, after seeing/listening to 'Paterson' for so long, memorizing every word of dialogue, of course, I became attached to the film

(notice how I didn't say obsessed) and it became, perhaps, my favorite film of all time (or at least a close second to Tornatore's 1988 masterpiece, 'Cinema Paradiso', that I only watch in the original Italian). And then something really interesting happened. It was September and a new customer booked a haircut, Michael was his name. Is his name. And when Michael walked into my shop that September evening, I nearly fell to the floor (maybe a bit exaggerated), but this guy was, maybe not your spitting image or twin brother separated at birth, but he looked enough like you to give me the heebie-jeebies; he was tall and thin, muscular; his hair was long and messy; his face chiseled and nose prominent and angular. Just like yours. Michael was also mild-mannered and soft-spoken; calm, cool and collected. Like Paterson or some of the other roles you played and how I imagined you might be in 'real life'. And more than anything, Michael—like you—reminded me of my son...My son. But that's another story for another day...I got home later that night and sat down at my computer and opened a new document and wrote out about a page of what became a movie treatment for a sequel to 'Paterson', I titled simply, 'A Return to Paterson'. I decided I really needed to see this film, even if it was only in my imagination or on my computer screen in a couple of loosely written pages. But the more I got into it, well, the more I got into it and by the time I got up from my computer it was nearly four a.m. and I had written a six-page treatment from beginning to end. And I'd never written a film treatment before; in fact, I'd never heard of a film treatment before I Googled 'how to write for films' like five minutes before I started writing the thing. It just came to me, the whole story. Paterson and Laura split up. Paterson publishes three collections of poetry that he'd been

sandbagging since his early twenties and when those blow
up he becomes the Poet Laureate of the State of New Jersey
and when the post is terminated by the governor, he's
appointed the Poet Laureate of the United States, the
youngest person ever appointed to that position. He moves
to D.C. and life goes on. Laura opens a chain of cupcake
shops then moves to Nashville, gets a record deal, releases a
hit single, opens more cupcake shops and life goes on. But as
time goes by, Paterson and Laura realize that their dreams
will never really mean anything without being able to share
them with the person who was the catalyst of those dreams
in the first place. So, they reunite and decide to give things
another go and the film ends when Paterson and Laura
show up at Doc's place one Sunday afternoon pushing a
double stroller and running into Everett and Marie who
announce their upcoming marriage with Marie visibly
pregnant. Then Donnie, Paterson's supervisor at the bus
depot enters the bar with Marvin and four little English
bulldog pups. Finally, Masatoshi Nagase, the Japanese actor
who portrayed the poet at the end of 'Paterson' walks into
the bar and, taking a line from the original film says,
'Excuse me, maybe not acceptable behavior, may I ask are
you knowing the great poet Paterson Hoeb here in Paterson,
New Jersey?' So, the implication is that in the original film
the Japanese poet asks Paterson if he knows the great poet
William Carlos Williams, who is a central figure—as is his
poetry—in the film. In the sequel's closing scene however, he
changes the name to Paterson's (rather than Williams)
while also revealing that Paterson was actually Paterson's
first name all along (something that is never revealed in the
original film as he's only ever referred to as Paterson). The
surname Hoeb, obviously, being my own invention. And the
cool part, though it's never mentioned in my sequel, is that

I chose Hoeb because it was the surname of William Carlos William's maternal grandparents, making Paterson (in my fantasy world) the last living descendant of Williams (I might just save that for 'Paterson 3!'). Then, Paterson and the Japanese poet embrace, while everyone mingles as Doc and his wife bring food and beverages out from behind the bar, setting them on long tables which have been decorated with flowers and balloons. Finally, as everyone is merrymaking, the Japanese poet taps a fork to his wine glass and the bar goes silent. Then, he says, 'Excuse me again,' pauses, and the entire cast, in loud voices, say (as the Japanese poet says in the film as he walks away), 'A-HA'! And the film ends.

In Charlie's Plan A, Driver speaks at that point, telling Charlie he loves the idea, asking him why he never tried to get the film made, to which Charlie tells him he has no idea of what he's been through and that the only way he saw getting his screenplay into the right hands was to get it into *his* (Adam Driver's) hands...

'What I could I possibly do?' asks Driver. 'Put up a million dollars to get the ball rolling', Charlie proclaimed; 'call Jim Jarmusch and the original cast members and get them all on board and let's make a movie'! 'So,' said Driver. 'That's the million-dollar haircut'. 'A-ha', replied Charlie.

By now, the audience is fully aware of what is going on and even more conscious of the fact that what they are witnessing is an extraordinary exchange between two complete strangers who, at face value, seem to be making a Hollywood movie deal right in the middle of a one-man show in an off-off-Broadway theater in New York City...

*'But', says Driver. 'But'? replies Charlie. 'I love the idea',
Driver continues, 'I mean I really love the idea and if I had
my check book in my pocket I'd write you a check right here
and now'. 'But'? asks Charlies again. 'But we're not going
to make a film', says Driver. 'Not make a film'? Charlie says,
confused. 'No', continues Driver. 'So, if we're not going to
make a film', Charlie follows, 'what are we going to make'?
'We', Driver says, 'are going to make a Broadway musical.
A big, juicy, blockbuster, Broadway musical'!*

Sadly, Plan A was never executed as Abbott, who had not
only been scanning the audience but actually went right up
to the lone figure at the back to get a close up look (under
the guise of asking the man to slightly move his chair to
the left for fire safety purposes). But it wasn't Driver,
though it fit the description fairly well, except for the fact
the young man seated there in the back row was at least ten
or fifteen years younger than Driver. As I sat in the barber
chair during the entire show, I wondered how Charlie was
feeling. There was nothing in his demeanor that suggested
he was anything but laser-focused and, now that I think
about in retrospect, it was by far the best performance out
of the five. In fact, after the curtain fell, the longer-than-
usual standing ovation segued into roaring chants of
Encore! Encore!! Utterly flabbergasted by the audience's
demand, Charlie simply looked over at Henny with a
bemused sort of smile on his face. Henny then started
playing the intro to *Phone Call, Phone Call*, the number
that show after show always received the longest ovation,
and the room quickly went from uproar to dead silence
and Charlie performed the song as the encore the audience
desired. Once the song finished, Charlie again was extolled

by the generosity of the audience with a standing ovation that tapered off as Charlie slowly walked off stage. As the house lights came up and the theater began emptying out, I noticed the man in the folding chair still seated. I was able to get an even better look at him now and I was surprised to see he actually did resemble Driver a bit, though his hair was just a shade lighter and he was obviously quite a bit younger, but could have passed for a brother or cousin as there was definitely an air of similarity. But why wasn't he getting up to leave, I wondered, as the last of the audience members walked past him and out the door. Just then, K. appeared from backstage, walked out into the house toward the man at the back, first shaking his hand then hugging him. K. and the man sat down and became engaged in conversation as my curiosity piqued. Not wanting K. to see me or be seen as a busybody, I walked back to the dressing room to find Charlie, Henny and his wife and Abbott and his daughter pouring Champagne. Charlie asked me if I'd seen K. and I said I think I might have seen her walking towards the toilets, but no sooner did I say that, the dressing room door opened and there stood K. with the young man beside her. Charlie slowly rose from his chair and took a few steps towards the door. He turned to us and, in a soft, breaking voice said, *'Everyone, I'd like you to meet my son, Aaron'*.

K., unbeknownst to Charlie, had arranged for Charlie's son to fly over from Spain and attend the closing night performance and reunite with his father, with whom he had not spoken to nor seen since the beginning of the pandemic. Charlie walked over and the two men embraced, tears flowing from their eyes and then from ours. We all filled our Champagne glasses and toasted Charlie and each other for an experience none of us would ever forget and then we filed out to the dressing room next door to give Charlie and his son some privacy and the time to get properly re-acquainted.

Charlie's son joined us for our closing night party at a place Charlie kept a secret the entire weekend. As we left the theater building we headed towards Times Square and found our way, following Charlie's lead, to the Knickerbocker Hotel where Charlie, in classic Charlie style, had rented out the lounge where they filmed the scene in *Marriage Story* where Adam Driver sang "Being Alive" from the musical *Company*. And the piano that was used in the scene was still there and after dinner Henny and Charlie performed a rendition of that song for us which brought us all to tears. Again. After dinner, dessert, dancing and drinks, the party broke up and we all returned to our hotels for our last sleep before flying back home on our nine-twenty-five p.m. flight to Amsterdam the following evening. But we still had a full day on Monday to enjoy the very best that New York City had to offer and we took full advantage of a beautiful sunny day in which to do so.

We met one last time for breakfast at Friedman's and then spent the day like the group of entitled tourists we were with our own personal tour guide, Jasmine, a lovely young woman who was an aspiring actor from Atlanta. We met Jasmine under the George M. Cohan statue on 46th and Broadway and from there enjoyed an action-packed day seeing all the sites and attractions you'd imagine such as St. Patrick's Cathedral, Grand Central Terminal, New York Stock Exchange, a subway trip and a semi-private tour of the MoMA, where we finished our day with an exquisite late *prix fixe* lunch at Chef Thomas Allan's restaurant The Modern, on the ground floor of the museum where I ate venison glazed in cognac with turnips and black truffle (that meal, I later found out, set Charlie back a hundred and fifty bucks a head!). After lunch, we went back to my hotel where everyone had checked their luggage, packed up the van and headed for JFK and our evening flight to Amsterdam.

During the seven-hour and twenty-minute flight, Charlie was quiet and pensive, though the expression on his face was one of contentedness. He listened to music or an audiobook for a bit and vacillated between conversations with K. and his son before getting up and stretching his legs in the aisle then coming over to where Henny, his wife and I sat a few rows behind. We chatted for a while before the cabin crew served a late-night meal and Charlie, who once told me that he could never sleep on airplane, fell fast asleep until breakfast was served somewhere over the west coast of Ireland.

We arrived in Amsterdam on a rainy morning, but the rain made me realize that I was home again. We boarded the Intercity train bound for The Hague and said our goodbyes at the central station before hopping trams for the last leg of our journeys home. I sat on the number nine tram looking out of the raindrop-covered window, my eyes adjusting to the brightness of the sun piercing through the white-clouded sky, my hearing still muffled from the flight and my heart filled with a joy I couldn't remember last experiencing. That it was me of all people that Charlie chose to confide in, to trust with his secret project and make me privy to his planning and every step of the development of his life's most important creative endeavor. And all because I pressed him for more—*how's the musical coming along? Any progress since I last saw you??*—and it was because I was truly interested in what

Charlie was doing, fascinated and maybe, if I'm to be completely honest, even a little envious that Charlie had lived his entire life doing exactly what he wanted to do, when and how he wanted to do it, and taking risks and suffering failures along the way. I, on the other hand, chose the safe route, the comfortable and convenient path. I went to law school like my father and his father and my brothers did. I joined the Marine Corp like they did, became a civil servant like they did and landed a job for life, a beautiful wife and loving children and all the things I could have ever dreamed of and truly appreciate. But deep inside, I've always longed for more, longed to be more like Charlie who went after the challenges and fought for every win and took every loss on the chin. They say the grass is always greener on the other side, but in Charlie's garden, the grass is as thick, green and plentiful as any can be.

In the days that followed our return to Holland, Charlie texted me nearly every day with funny quips, quotes, photos from New York, a wide assortment of links to irrelevant TikTok videos, Instagram stories and Facebook memes. I guess I could say that was Charlie's way of confirming what I had felt for some time, that we were becoming good friends. And Charlie was, and is, a good friend. The next time I saw Charlie was at the barbershop about a week later. I had booked a haircut after work and arrived a few minutes early to find Charlie sweeping up and oiling his clippers, *The Ghost in You* by the Psychedelic Furs playing on the Bluetooth speakers. Charlie looked up and saw me and walked right over to greet me, taking his phone out of the back pocket of his 501s.

"You're not going believe this," Charlie said with nine out ten excitement. "It's an email from Abbott in Zurich.

Well, it's a forwarded email from Abbott that his daughter in New York sent him this morning. It's a clipping from an article by Adam Feldman, who covers the off-off-Broadway beat for *Time Out* magazine."

"A review? I asked.

"Not exactly. It's a man-in-the-street piece where Feldman asks random people if they'd seen any off-off productions in the past six months and what their reaction was. One woman, wait, let's see, a woman named Jane, 32, a seamstress in the theater sector, said she'd seen an unusual one-man musical named *Adam Driver and the Million Dollar Haircut* at the Sargent…"

"Unusual? That's good right…?"

"There's more," said Charlie. "The actor was a 60-something-year-old man who rifled through a series of stories about how his own life had somehow become intertwined with characters Adam Driver played in some of his films and how the man had tried to get a screenplay he wrote as a sequel to one of Driver's more obscure films, *Paterson*, made into an actual movie."

"That sounds a little review-ish to me," I interrupted.

"Yeah, I know," Charlie said. "I think it's Feldman paraphrasing. Wait, listen to this, this is Feldman writing, he says, 'Jane was not the first person I met during my week in the streets talking to New York theatergoers who mentioned this particular show, and as I became more and more intrigued about it I decided to look into this one-off, three-day run at the Sargent Theatre in the A.T.A. complex on West 54th Street and was surprised to have found very little about the play, the playwright or producers of the show. What I did do was reach out to Adam Driver's people who said they'd heard about the play but that Driver was abroad and unavailable for comment. For next month's article, I'll try to unravel this mystery play a bit more.'"

"Wow! That's incredible," I said. "You know what that could mean?"

"I do," Charlie replied. "It could mean I finally get my screenplay into the right hands."

"Yes," I agreed. But remember, you wrote, produced, composed and acted in a one-man musical in New York City!"

Charlie nodded as he read the rest of Abbott's email and gestured for me to sit in his chair while he tapped out a quick reply on his smartphone. During my forty-five-minute haircut, it was classic Charlie, telling me about how things ended up with his son, who stayed in The Hague visiting his sisters for a few days before flying back to Valencia, and how K. arranged the whole thing without ever giving any indication of what she was up to, coordinating everything with her stepson and spending more than a few hours talking to him by phone and on WhatsApp. And she paid for everything, the flights, hotel, meals and even gave him spending money, which he humbly accepted. Charlie had something new and exciting to look forward to and he thought about reaching out to the journalist, Feldman, to see if he could land an interview or at least make his acquaintance and tell him his story and how Adam Driver figured into the scheme of things. But before Charlie even had the chance to give it another thought, he received an email from Feldman himself:

Hey Charlie!

My name is Adam Feldman, I'm the theater and cabaret critic for *Time Out New York*. Last week I published an article about off-off-Broadway plays and a few people I interviewed for the piece said they'd seen your show at the Sargent and really loved it. I have to admit I saw the play listed in the agenda and the title really caught my eye, but as I rarely review any off-off shows these days, I put it in the back of my mind and now regret doing so. Want to grab a coffee later this week? I'd love to hear more about your play. Will you be putting it up again somewhere sometime soon?

Thanks,
A.F.

Charlie was flabbergasted to receive that email and responded at the first chance he got:

Hey Adam!

Thank you so much for reaching out! I saw your piece as my director's daughter came upon it online and sent it my way. I'd love to grab coffee, but I live in the Netherlands, so perhaps we could do a FaceTime one of these days unless you've got Holland on your travel agenda! As far as another run for my show, it's Broadway or bust, but so far the offers haven't starting flooding in!!

Thanks again,
Charlie

Charlie considered this out-of-the-blue new relationship with Feldman to be an omen and perhaps a way for Charlie to take his project to new heights. What if this Feldman turns out to be a champion? What if he would have seen the show, loved it and gave it a raving review?? And what a great human-interest story—the sixty-something, former teacher turned barber turned theater maker, now that's what readers want to read about. And what if Charlie's dream of getting his movie made or having the one-man show become a real Broadway musical with a full cast, chorus line, orchestra and all the hoopla really came to be thanks to this Feldman??? More than anyone, maybe even more than K., who came to the Charlie party late, I thought I really knew Charlie and there was one thing that always bothered me, a darker side to the bright and shining sun that has always been the Charlie I've known. Charlie, though he doesn't talk about it often, and when he does it's in a fleeting and glossed over way, is preoccupied with mortality—his mortality. He often jokes about being a hypochondriac and though I only recall him having a few colds or bouts of allergies and asthma during the spring, I've always thought of Charlie as being the picture of health; why, he never even got COVID, he eats well, gets his rest, takes a handful of daily supplements and still wears a mask at work and on public transportation despite the pandemic being far behind us. *I think I'm more susceptible to colds and flu*, Charlie would say; *and as a barber, it's a close-contact profession, like a dentist, and they mask up so why shouldn't I?*

But as time went by, Charlie talked more about aging, the aches and pains, the joint stiffness and the myriad of doleful feelings and premonitions that would come and go leaving him emotionally drained, anxious and depressed. He worried about an apocalypse, some natural disaster in which the world was bombarded with deadly gamma rays and he worried that if such an event would occur while his children were at school they would perish frightened and alone and that idea tormented Charlie. Likewise, he feared dying alone and his children hearing the news from a voice on the phone or text message. And he was always afraid that a plane would crash into his duplex as it sat on the third and fourth floors above the street and was situated on the flight path of planes coming from the south preparing to land at Amsterdam's Schiphol Airport (it always reminded him of a scene in one his favorite films, *The World According to Garp*, based on the novel of the same name by one of his favorite American novelists John Irving. In the film, Garp, played by Robin Williams in one of his first leading film roles, is standing in front a house he and his wife are interested in buying when a distressed propeller plane crashes into the roof and Garp proclaims "we'll take the house…the chances of another plane hitting this house are astronomical…it's been pre-disastered!"). So, Charlie, like most of us, lives with a plethora of fears— legitimate, unfounded or otherwise—and at times they really seem to consume him. But as far as I'm concerned— and I'm certainly no expert on psychology—Charlie is one of the most well-balanced and mentally-sound people I've ever known. Furthermore, if I look as good as he does when I'm in my sixties, I'll be a very happy man indeed.

Charlie continued running The Night Barber and soon there were eight franchises, the newest in Paris. And while the day-to-day operations were being managed by Charlie and K. and their Ukrainian accountant Chanel, and Charlie no longer needed to work, he continued going into the shop a few times a month to see his regulars and chat with the guys as he still loved barbering and soaking up the vibe at the shop. He also traveled occasionally to the shops in London, Brussels, Madrid and Lisbon to check in on things and talk with the barbers about this and that, bringing in lunch and showing he was interested in more than just business, that he truly cared about the people who were carrying on his legacy.

After a short hiatus, Charlie and Henny were back to rehearsing and Abbott flew in from Zurich to fine-tune the latest version of the show, which now included three new songs and about fifteen minutes of new material, taking the running time to ninety minutes. Henny hired a fellow Ukrainian musician who arranged parts for horns, strings and percussion. For shows at larger venues, which were being booked more frequently, Henny led a six-piece ensemble that added an amazing new dimension to the show which, more and more, was starting to feel like a real Broadway production. And Broadway—well, close enough for jazz Broadway—would indeed be in Charlie's future as, just like I imagined would happen, that theater critic Adam Feldman did become a champion and an early backer of the musical that would eventually open, not on Broadway, but on the mainstage at Playwrights Horizon, a 198-seat theater on West 42nd Street. The musical, in two acts, was a hybrid of the one-man show—the barbershop, the stories, the songs, etcetera. My muted barbershop chair customer even became a speaking part, a character Charlie named Jasper (to protect my privacy, he told me!). By the end of act one, he had Adam Driver (not the real Adam Driver obviously) sitting in his chair, getting an earful of Charlie's spiel and, ta-da! Driver agrees to bankroll the project—the sequel to *Paterson*—not as a film, but as a Broadway musical! Act one closes with a musical number performed by Charlie and the Adam Driver character and as the curtain goes up on act two, the stage is now divided into a four-part, moveable, diorama-like stage featuring the recording studio where Laura records, Paterson's Washington, D.C. apartment, Laura and Paterson's New Jersey home and Doc's bar, Shades, back in Paterson. The action shifts between the different scenes and musical numbers are interspersed, some as solos and others as duets sung by Paterson and Laura. While I'd like to tell you that the show was a big hit—it did get some very good reviews—it ran into a major setback just a week into its projected three-month run. But not for the reasons a play usually encounters problems...

On the seventh day of the run, K. arrived at the theater while Charlie was meeting with the technical director to go over a few lighting changes. She signaled for Charlie to come over and the two went into Charlie's dressing room.

"This letter arrived at the apartment by messenger about thirty minutes ago," said K. obviously distraught by its contents.

Charlie opened the envelope and in it was a letter from Chasen, Whitehouse and Gould, one of New York's top law firms. It was a cease and desist letter ordering the immediate closure of Charlie's play. And who would, and why, send such a letter? Charlie read on and when he saw the complainant's name he was shocked to see it was none other than Jim Jarmusch, the same Jim Jarmusch who wrote and directed *Paterson*. In the complaint, Jarmusch accuses Charlie of copyright infringement, amongst other things. Here is that letter:

To the Producers of *Adam Driver and the Million Dollar Haircut*:

I am writing to you on behalf of James Robert Jarmusch, the rightful owner of the intellectual property associated with the film *Paterson*. It has come to our attention that you have engaged in the unauthorized use of characters and storylines from *Paterson* in your recent above-mentioned musical production. This infringement is a blatant violation of our client's exclusive rights as the creator of the original material, therefore, we hereby demand that you cease and desist from any further use or public display of the characters and storylines from *Paterson* effective immediately. Failure to comply with this demand will leave us with no choice but to pursue legal action to protect our client's rights under intellectual property laws. We strongly advise you to seek legal counsel to understand the gravity of the situation and the potential consequences of your actions. Our client is prepared to take all necessary steps to enforce their rights and seek appropriate remedies for the damages incurred. This letter is not exhaustive of our client's rights, remedies, claims, or defenses, all of which are expressly reserved.

Sincerely,
Siobhan Goosen
Chasen, Whitehouse & Gould, LLP
1251 Avenue of the Americas
New York, NY 10020

Charlie's mouth dropped to the floor as he read the letter.

"How could this have happened?" said Charlie. "We cleared everything with our people and they said not only would there not be any infringement, he said that we were covered by our disclaimer that some characters in the presentation were based on characters created by Jim Jarmusch. That's all we needed to do, they said"

But it turned out there may have been additional infringements on Jarmusch's intellectual property and he had every right to seek legal counsel and have the show brought to a grinding halt, at least until there was some sort of communication between the parties involved.

"What if you change the names of the characters?" asked K.

"Well, I suppose I could do that," replied Charlie. "But I think the story wouldn't make sense anymore."

Charlie immediately got on the phone and called his New York attorney Brendan Rushakoff, who said he'd meet Charlie and K. at the theater in thirty minutes, that he shouldn't worry and wait for him to sort things out. When Brendan arrived, he told Charlie he'd put a call into the law firm while he was driving over in a taxi and that there was probably nothing that could be done before the show that evening and that the performance would have to be canceled and refunds issued. Charlie was distraught and had to get on the phone immediately to begin the dire task of informing the cast about the bad news and convey what was happening to the theater manager. In the end, Charlie decided that a long-drawn out court battle with someone like Jim Jarmusch, who certainly had the financial resources should there be a protracted court case, wouldn't be worth the time or expense and he made the heart-wrenching decision to close down the show, using the insurance money to pay off the actor's contracts, ticket refunds and the balance of what the production owed the theater. Charlie's Broadway dream had been deflated and he was inconsolable. But that's hardly where the story ends...

CHAPTER FIVE

AUSTIN, TEXAS

I've learned many things from Charlie over the past few years that I've known him and been part of his inner circle, if you would, and I suppose I could say that the most important lesson was how to keep cool in the face of adversity. I think anyone else in Charlie's shoes during that time in New York when the show got canceled would have reacted differently. But Charlie kept his wits about him and kept saying things like, *if it was meant to be, then, let it be*; or, *if that's what fate had in store...*

Charlie's New York lawyer Brendan Rushakoff arrived at the theater and made a flurry of calls, first and foremost to the law firm representing Jim Jarmusch, who had sent the cease and desist letter, then to his office to get his associates working on an injunction to postpone the immediate cessation of the production while Brendan could get legal proceedings underway. Here's where the story really gets good...While Brendan's on the phone and Charlie is pacing back and forth in his small dressing room, he gets a call from the theater office saying there is someone asking for him. Charlie says to send the visitor to the dressing room and two minutes later the door opens and standing there, wearing a long black raincoat and vintage Ray-Ban Aviators, is Jim Jarmusch himself. In the flesh.

"You must be Charlie," Jarmusch says, extending a hand.

"That's right, I'm Charlie," he responds slowing edging his hand toward Jarmusch's with a look of total surprise and barely able to come up with another word. "Are you…"

"—Jim Jarmusch, very nice to meet you. I apologize for barging in, I know you have a show to get ready for, but I was trying to fend off a bit of a…well…a bit of a situation and I thought that coming over in person would be better than just calling."

"Fending off a situation?" Charlie said, still clutching Jarmusch's hand in his.

"I got a text from my lawyer this morning and I was in a meeting with some suits and told him I couldn't respond and that whatever he wanted to just go ahead and do it and fill me in later. While I was having lunch with these Hollywood monkeys, I got another text message with the cease and desist letter and it was the first thing I'd ever heard about it. I mean, I knew about your play—from Adam—"

"Adam?" asked Charlie, finally letting go of Jarmusch's hand, his eyes opening so wide his eyeballs nearly popped out of their sockets.

"Yeah," replied Jarmusch. "Adam Feldman, you know him, the *Time Out* guy. He said the show was pretty amazing," he continued, reaching into the inside pocket of his raincoat pulling out a small envelope. "I even got tickets for tonight's show for me, Sara and Adam."

"Adam?" Charlie asked, this time with greater enthusiasm.

"Feldman," replied Jarmusch.

"Of course, Feldman," said Charlie. "So, you mean I can do the show tonight?"

"Of course," answered Jarmusch. "Tonight and every night. And I'm really sorry about the miscommunication, you know how these big shot lawyers can be real assholes sometimes."

"I do," said Charlie, looking over at Brendan, who was nodding his head with a boyish grin. "Oh, I'm sorry, Jim, this my attorney Brendan Rushakoff and my wife K."

"Nice to meet you both," said Jarmusch, extending a hand to greet them. "Rushakoff?" continued Jarmusch. "Any relation to Harry, the drummer in Concrete Blonde?"

"He's a cousin, actually," said Brendan. "From the Chicago Rushakoffs. Charlie here grew up in the same neighborhood as Harry."

"I've known him for fifty years," added Charlie.

"*Walking in London*," said Jarmusch, "is one my favorite albums. That guy can really kick out a beat, and that snare sound! Anyway, I don't want to keep you and I'm meeting Sara and Adam for dinner. Nice meeting everyone and I'm sorry again about the cock-up. And break a leg tonight, Charlie."

Charlie stood at the dressing room door as Jim Jarmusch walked away, then turned to K. and Brendan looking slightly perplexed with a did-that-really-happen expression on his face. Then, the three of them broke out into a fit of giggles, Charlie with tears streaming from his eyes and a laugh, as it tends to do, turning into a hysterical and infectious bout of coughing and wheezing that lasts long after anyone else in his presence has calmed down. I've only had the privilege (if you could call it that) of actually being present once during one of Charlie's laugh attacks and it's surely a rare event to behold.

After the show, while Charlie was tidying up his dressing room, Jim Jarmusch, his partner, filmmaker and actress Sara Driver (I know, right?) and Adam Feldman appeared at the door. Charlie welcomed them in and Jarmusch asked if Charlie would like to join them at Shark Bar (as the Spring Lounge on Spring and Mulberry on the Lower East Side is more popularly called due to the many sharks placed about the establishment). Charlie obliged and rang K., who was already waiting outside, to tell her about their invitation and, in two yellow cabs, the group made their way to the Lower East Side.

At Shark Bar, Charlie tried to hold it together as the elation of clinking glasses with Jim Jarmusch and *his people* was a big emotional load, feeling both star-struck and blessed to be where he was with who he was trying to live in the moment of one of his life's truly most amazing moments. They started off with two bottles of Lamberti Rosé Prosecco that seemed to appear magically at the table before jackets had even found their way to the backs of chairs. Once seated and glasses filled, Jarmusch raised his and proposed a toast:

"To our new friend, Charlie the barber and to new frontiers."

What did he mean by *new frontiers*? Charlie asked himself as the idea of him now being friends with Jim Jarmusch was starting to sink in.

"You know, Charlie," said Jarmusch, "I lived in Chicago for a while in the early 70s, studied at Northwestern. Great town, Chicago. Get back there much?"

"Well," answered Charlie." "Actually, I haven't been home since June of 1998"

"O-kay," said Jarmusch, his eyes opening wide with surprise. "You a wanted man?" joked Jarmusch.

"Well, not really," said Charlie. "But there was this little bank heist, but I won't bore you with the details."

"You hear that?" barked Jarmusch. "A little bank heist, I like that, good midwestern humor. You know, people think Midwesterners don't have a sense of humor," he continued. "A little bank heist. Love it!"

The two men shared a hearty laugh and Charlie filled everyone's glasses as genteel conversation carried on well into the night. Just after one a.m., when the fourth bottle of Prosecco ran dry, Jarmusch stood up and walked over to the bar where the owner Bryan Delaney was pulling a beer and ordered six jiggers of Balvenie Single Malt Scotch, carrying them back to the table on a small tray, sticky from spilled beer. After the Scotch in the second round of jiggers was sipped, Jarmusch knocked his knuckles on the table.

"Okay, so, how does this sound to you K.," Jarmusch said, turning his chair and attention toward her. "Your husband and I are going to make little film…"

As those words fell from the director's mouth, Charlie's heart fell into his stomach and all he could muster up was a tiny toothy grin.

"Now, you may or may not know this, but I've directed thirteen films, and do you know how many of those thirteen films I've written?"

"Thirteen?" answered K. with raised eyebrows.

"Exactly, thirteen," confirmed Jarmusch. "Now I have a place up in the Catskills—tranquil, beautiful views—and I'm going to move you and your husband into that beautiful and tranquil house—you'll have everything you need and all the privacy you could ask for—and I'm going to do something I've never done—said I'd never do because it was never really something I set out to do or wanted to do. And do you know what that might be, K?"

"Uhh…" replied K. "Make a film with someone?"

"Exactly! Make a film with someone. So, what do you say, K.? You think your husband would go along with that?"

"Well," answered K. "He is sitting right there after all."

"He is, isn't he," said Jarmusch. "So, what do say, Charlie the barber? You up to making a film?"

Charlie was flabbergasted and the two men laid out a game plan on the back of two coasters. First, Jarmusch needed to reach out to his friends Josh Astrachan and Carter Logan, who produced *Paterson*, and cinematographer Frederick Elmes, who'd worked on five of Jarmusch's films. Once he got his production team in place, he would, methodically, one by one, contact each of the original film's cast members who would feature in Charlie's sequel. There was just one potential complication, Jarmusch said to Charlie and K.

"Okay, so that's the timeline and the basic way that I see things coming to together," said Jarmusch, fanning himself with the coasters which now contained the master plan written on them. "But, there is one question mark," he continued.

"Question mark?" asked Charlie.

"Well," said Jarmusch, "maybe just like one of those upside-down Spanish question marks."

"*Bueno*," said Charlie. "*¿Qué pasa?*"

"So," continued Jarmusch. "I had a chat with Adam—Driver—just this morning."

"Okay," said Charlie reflectively. "And…?"

"And he's not exactly what you would call on board with the project."

"I see," said Charlie. "So, what does that mean?"

"It means *you'll* have to convince him," said Jarmusch in a very matter-of-fact sort of way."

"*I'll* have to convince Adam Driver to come on board?" asked Charlie in a downtrodden tone.

"He's out in Austin with Jeff Nichols who's been trying to make this Cuban Revolution film for years now and if that comes off, we might have timeline problems. That's why *you* should talk to Adam."

"Talk to him about what?" asked Charlie.

"Adam's a bit, well, what you might call…particular."

"Particular?" repeated Charlie.

"Let me be direct. He doesn't really like sequels. Hates them. Passionately."

"And *Star Wars*?" Charlie countered.

"*Star Wars* is a paycheck," Jarmusch rejoined.

So, Adam Driver was a holdout it seemed and it would be left up to Charlie to plead his case. And that terrified Charlie. Not only had he never met Driver, but now he was made fully aware that Driver knew of him and his project. Surely, he would been party to all the effort Charlie had been making over the past few years to get the actor's attention. After all, he wrote a musical with the actor's name in the title! "What would Driver think about Charlie?" he wondered. Maybe he'd see him as a sycophant, some crazed fan who writes a screenplay for the actor he obsesses over just to try and get close to him. That bothered Charlie who, while he did admire Driver as an actor, wasn't the obsessed fan type. If indeed there was any obsession on Charlie's behalf, it was with *Paterson*, the film, and wanting to see a sequel that brought closure to the lives of the characters from his favorite movie of all time.

On the following Monday, Charlie boarded an early morning flight and flew to Austin, arriving just as the sun was coming up, to meet Adam Driver, the movie star. The two met at Pacha Organic Cafe on Guadalupe Street where Charlie ordered a grilled vegan platter and a stack of pancakes. Driver ordered a granola bowl and a one-yoke, six egg white omelet that didn't even make the waitress flinch. It was a pleasant and cordial meeting; Driver was just as down to earth as Charlie had always imagined he would be and went out of his way to make Charlie feel at ease. Driver had a million questions but, to Charlie's surprise, none of them had anything to do with Charlie's screenplay and were more about Charlie himself. Driver, the consummate actor, was more enthralled by Charlie's personal story—teacher, barber, bow tie maker, father, playwright and cabaret performer (as Driver referred to Charlie)—than merely talking shop (he did plenty of that at his day job). Driver was particularly interested in knowing all about Charlie fronting a new wave band in L.A. in the 1980s, which he was fascinated by. After more than two hours and countless coffee refills, Driver looked at his watch and said he had to get back to another meeting at Jeff Nichol's place before flying back to New York early that evening. And without any mention of the sequel, Driver slipped a fifty-dollar bill under his coffee mug, gave Charlie a hearty handshake and said he hoped to see Charlie again soon. And just like that, Driver was gone and Charlie sat there at the table in a near state of bewilderment. He had just met—no, not just met—just had breakfast with Adam Driver, the same Adam Driver he had flown seventeen hundred miles to convince to star in the sequel to *Paterson*. And in all the time he had spent eating and talking and drinking coffee with the movie star, the sequel never even came up.

Completely dispirited, Charlie drove his rental car over to the Holiday Inn on Middle Fiskville Road and told the receptionist he wouldn't be checking in and was returning to New York on the next flight out. The young man at reception was very accommodating and told Charlie he would cancel the reservation without penalty and wished Charlie a safe trip back east. Charlie returned the car and walked into the airport and over to the ticket counter to change his return flight, but the next flight wasn't until seven p.m., so he decided to go through security and hunker down at the Haymaker, where he plugged in his devices and got onto his laptop to check his emails and social media accounts. The afternoon slowly passed and Charlie had an Impossible burger with a side of coleslaw for his late lunch and then found a comfortable chair near the gate, called K. and the kids, took a fifteen-minute power nap then watched *Paterson* (for the umpteenth time) on his MacBook. About an hour before boarding, Charlie heard a familiar voice talking on a cellphone nearby. He turned around and, sure as eggs is eggs, it was Adam Driver sitting behind him on the opposite row of chairs. Once Charlie heard Driver end the call, he walked around and greeted the actor, who was pleasantly surprised to see his new friend and breakfast companion. Charlie and Driver were on the same flight back to JFK and the actor abandoned his business-class seat to spend the three-hour and forty-minute flight sitting with Charlie in economy on the sparsely booked flight, and just minutes after take-off, Driver turned to Charlie, lifted the armrest in the middle seat, crossed his long legs and, to Charlie's surprise, began talking about the sequel.

"So," said Driver, lowering the tray table and resting his arm on it. "Jim tells me you wanted to talk to me about your screenplay, and I'm sorry it didn't come up at breakfast this morning but my head was in two places and I was so focused on your stories that the screenplay totally slipped my mind. And of course, I had meant to mention how much I enjoyed your show at the Sargent, when was it, year before last?"

"You saw my show at the Sargent?" asked Charlie in disbelief.

"Sure," said Driver. "You sent me a press kit and a couple of tickets. I was there on closing night and when I asked someone if you were available they told me something about your son having flown in from Spain and that you hadn't seen him in a while or something like that and I didn't want to intrude."

Charlie smiled and nodded though he couldn't believe what Driver had just told him. He was there on closing night at the Sargent, the night his son was there and no one saw him, no one recognized Adam Driver in a small crowd in a small theater? For the next hour, Driver sat quietly, hanging on Charlie's every word as he explained in detail the story of *A Return to Paterson*. As the plane was on its final approach into JFK, Driver put his tray table up, clicked his seatbelt in and turned to Charlie.

"I love the story," Driver said to Charlie. "And you know something, I loved making that film, especially because it was a nice change from what I'd been doing that year; made two heavy films, *Midnight Special* with Jeff and the Scorsese film, *Silence*. And the year before was *Star Wars*, so there was still a lot of hype and promo and I'd be flying everywhere, like twenty hours to do a dozen five-minute interviews. All that while making three films that year. But *Paterson* was a respite, actually gave me some time to clear my head. We filmed in the fall and those thirty days were heaven and because it was a small cast and small production, we all got pretty close on that film, it was like making a movie with your high school friends. And you know something, we actually talked about a sequel, yeah, just joking around, but one day I said to Jim that Paterson and Laura should have started a lounge act, performing together at Doc's. I mean, Golshifteh can sing, I mean really sing, and I play piano and while I don't sing that often—and I'm never all that keen to sing on film, though I've done it, reluctantly—it would have been great to see that happen but Jim just laughed it off and we never talked about again."

The plane landed and there was a delay getting to the gate, but what happened in the twenty or so minutes the plane was taxiing would change Charlie's life—and the dream of getting his screenplay made into film—forever. Driver reiterated how much he loved the idea of Charlie's *Paterson* sequel, but what he said to Charlie was something he could have never imagined…

"I love your concept, Charlie, and I'm in," said Driver nonchalantly, taking a sip of water from the metal water bottle he pulled out of his backpack.

"You're in?" repeated Charlie trying to mask the sound disbelief in his voice.

"I'll make the first move, financially that is, so I'll wear a producer's hat; that'll help get the ball rolling and give me a bit of leeway; and I know Jim's on board and already talking to people. But there's one thing…"

"One thing?" asked Charlie.

"One thing, but promise me you'll hear me out before saying anything."

"Sure, of course," said Charlie.

"I'll bankroll my share, produce, play Paterson, of course, do my best to do whatever I can to get this off the ground, but we won't be making a film and you have to trust me on that."

"Not be making a film?" said Charlie.

"No film," replied Driver.

"But you just said—"

"I know what I said," interrupted Driver. We're making your sequel but it's not going to be a film."

"Then what?" asked Charlie, bewildered and curious.

"*A Return to Paterson* is going to be a musical, a big, fat, juicy, over-the-top, brilliant Broadway musical! I mean, what better thing? Your scenes with Paterson and Laura in the play are great, and that ending at Doc's, where everybody shows up—the Japanese poet—awesome! Look Charlie, films are great, we know that, but theater is where it's at and to be honest, I think your story was made for the stage—you studied playwriting, right?—You're a playwright and your story, as well as it would translate to film, is perfect for the stage, perfect for a full cast, orchestra and chorus line—just like you talked about in your show."

"But what about Jim?" asked Charlie.

"Jim loves the idea," said Driver. "I called him after we had breakfast, woke him up and everything! He's been wanting to direct a Broadway show for as long as I've known him; well, secretly anyway, he's funny about his filmmaker's mystique and all that, but when I told him about doing the sequel as a musical, he laughed hysterically and said 'if you can make it work, I'm in.' So, are *you* in, Charlie?"

Charlie was in alright, and during the taxi ride that Charlie and Driver shared into town from the airport, calls were made, balls were set a-rolling, chuckles were chuckled and two men who were little more than strangers just hours earlier having breakfast together at a café in Austin, Texas, were making plans for the future, one that was as bright as the lights on a Broadway marquee. And while Charlie never did get Adam Driver in his barber chair or give the movie star a haircut as he had desired to do, an envelope with a return address of *A.D., Paterson, NJ*, arrived for Charlie a few days later at the theater. I imagine you can guess what was inside…

In Memoriam

Cornelius Bumpus
Eugene Canning
Linda Carson Miller
Anthony Crippin
Scott Metcalfe
Ronald Weiss

Printed in Great Britain
by Amazon

45966492R00108